Outback *Hearts*

By Susan Stoker

Diane -
Being true to
yourself always
wins out in the
end! ☺

Susan Stoker

1

Susan Stoker

This is a work of fiction. Names, characters, places and incidents are either the product of the author's imagination or used fictitiously, and any resemblance to actual persons, living or dead, business establishments, events or locales is entirely coincidental.

ISBN-13:978-1500776541
ISBN-10:1500776548

Published by Beau Coup Publishing
http://beaucoupllc.com

Cover by JRA Stevens
For Beau Coup Publishing

Susan Stoker

Chapter One

How in the world did I end up here? Sam thought to herself.

'Here' was Australia, the 'Outback' more specifically. It was almost a year ago that an article in the local paper announced there was going to be a new reality show set in the Australian Outback and they were looking for twenty to thirty-five-year-old women to audition. The ad was pretty vague and didn't say what the show was going to be about. Beth had found the ad and one night, over several Margaritas, Sam, Beth, and Christina had sat down together and each had filled out an application. It was a lark, something that they did for "fun." The ad requested that each application had to be accompanied by a headshot and a full body shot picture. They figured since it was for television they wanted to make sure they didn't have any really ugly people picked. Months went by and all three had forgotten about the applications.

Then a couple of months ago Sam got the phone call. It was the producers informing her that she'd been chosen to come in and interview in person. When she showed up, there were about one hundred other women there. Most of them looked like models. Sam had always been self-conscious about her weight. Beth and Christina were both slender. Beth was about five feet ten inches tall and Christina was a very petite five feet three inches. Sam was an average five feet six inches and weighed about one hundred and fifty pounds. She wasn't really fat, but she also wasn't skinny either. So she figured that with all these model look-alikes there was no way that she was going to make it to the next round…but after a panel interview, a group interview with some of the other perspective contestants, a one-on-one interview with a psychologist, and a thorough medical exam…it turned out that she was one of sixteen women chosen for the show. And they still hadn't really said what the show was going to be about.

So, here I am. Sam thought. She'd taken two months' leave at her job—luckily, she had a great boss and lots of leave saved up—and gotten on a plane to the Outback. The producers hadn't told her much about the trip, except that there might be some camping involved. Sam had seen enough reality shows in her lifetime to know that "some" camping probably meant that they would be spending the entire time in the wilds of the Outback. She thought back to that reality show a few years back where one guy "Jack"—*which wasn't even his real nam*e, she thought to herself with disgust—had to pick from a bunch of spoiled rotten debutants which one he wanted to spend the rest of his life with. She, Beth, and Christina had watched the show and laughed at all the women who complained about where to plug in their hairdryers and about the icky bugs. They couldn't see why anyone would want to degrade themselves to be on that show and they didn't understand how "Jack" could see past all of the "glamour" to really get to know any of the women.

Sam loved camping and didn't mind—indeed hoped—that they'd get to spend some time outside, communing with nature. She didn't mind being dirty and loved being outside. So with that in mind she packed a carry-on suitcase full of clothes and another backpack with essentials.

Sam was brought to a hotel room from the plane and told that tomorrow she would meet the other contestants and the next day their adventure would start. She was handed a packet of information about the show and the "rules" they had to follow. Her name was written on the packet, but instead of Sam, her name was written "Sammi." When she asked about it she was told that it was just a part of the show.

Sam sat down to read the information she'd been given. The notes on the show were short and vague:

You have been chosen as one of sixteen women to be on a reality show about dating, love, and real life. One by one, contestants will leave the show until there is only one left. You are not allowed to ask to be kicked off. The last remaining contestant will win.

And that was all it said.

"Whatever," Sam mumbled to herself. They were certainly being as vague as possible about the whole thing. Sam was a bit cautious and suspicious in nature. She remembered the other reality show she and her friends had watched, where the entire show was a lie. There was only one person who didn't know, and it was all based around him. She wondered if this was the case here as well. Now that she thought about it there was another reality show where the women went to Vegas and the rich man got to choose one of them for his wife and they had to get married right there on the show. Of course, it ended badly. Sam remembered an interview with that "winner" saying she'd agreed to be a contestant because she wanted a free trip to Las Vegas. Sam hoped that wasn't what she'd gotten herself into. Sam went on to read the "rules" of the show. They went on for pages and pages, most of which were legal things like "contestants aren't allowed to agree to share any prizes" and things like that. There were also things like "contestants will agree to be taped at all times and will not engage camera personnel in conversation." Sam thought to herself, *this sounds more and more like* Survivor. She figured there wasn't anything more that she could do tonight and decided not to worry about it until tomorrow.

Chapter Two

Sam got dressed in a pair of jeans and a V-neck sweater, then put on the nametag that was included in the packet she received the night before, and winced. She still didn't like the fact that she had to go by "Sammi." She hadn't been called Sammi since she was twelve years old and she moved to a different school. She'd decided it was more "grown-up" to be called Sam.

She entered the ballroom in the hotel and saw there weren't that many people there yet. There were little cocktail tables evenly set up around the room, as well as a bar in the corner. A few people were milling around and clustered in groups, talking. Sam had never been comfortable just walking up to people and talking, so she went to get a soft drink from the bartender and sat at one of the little tables.

The room quickly started filling up. The women who were wearing nametags were all beautiful. Most were tall. All of them could have been models. For what seemed like the hundredth time, Sam mumbled, "What am I doing here?" She didn't belong. She knew it, and it seemed like everyone else in the room knew it also. They'd see her and then do a double take as if to make sure they were seeing her correctly. Sam immediately knew she wasn't wearing the appropriate outfit. Most of the other contestants were wearing short skirts or dresses, with their hair in fancy upsweeps and perfect made up faces. Sam knew this was going to go badly.

9

Soon one of the producers got up on the podium in the front of the room. He seemed to be the person in charge. Sammi remembered he'd introduced himself to her as Eddie.

Eddie dramatically announced, "Welcome to the Outback. We are so pleased to have you all here. We know that this is going to be the best reality show to air on television back in the States and you're all going to be stars!"

At that, the room broke out into spontaneous cheering and clapping.

Oh brother, Sam thought, this is really over the top.

Eddie on the podium continued, "I'd like to take this time to introduce all of our lovely contestants..."

With that he started calling the women up to the stage one by one. "Katie from New York City, Brandi from Phoenix, Kimmie from San Diego, Ashley from Toledo, Cindee from Albany, Lori from Colorado Springs, KiKi from Miami, Courtnee from Pensacola..."

Sam was starting to feel a little sick. All the women were lining up on stage and it seemed like they were automatically doing the "pageant pose" where one leg was a bit forward, their hips were swiveled, and their hands were on their hips. Most of them had long hair that was either flowing around their shoulders or up in an elegant updo. The man continued...

"Candi from Greensboro, Jennie from Billings, Missy from Los Angeles, Sammi from Albuquerque..."

Sam walked up on stage and stood next to Missy.

She felt very awkward and out of place. She was a bit shorter than Missy and weighed about thirty pounds more. She felt like a beached whale next to all the other women. She knew she wasn't obese. In fact, she was probably the most normal sized woman there, but compared to the others she definitely stood out. Missy was wearing a white miniskirt which showed off her mile long legs. Sam wondered if she'd even remembered to shave her legs before getting on the plane. She had to remember to shave tonight before the show started, just in case.

"Wendi from Las Vegas, Nikki from Seattle, Amy from El Paso, and last but not least Kathi from Knoxville. Remember these faces, everyone, these are our new contestants for our show called "Love in the Outback.""

It was even worse than she could imagine. Love in the Outback?!? Barf. Hopefully they would reconsider that name before this stupid show ever aired. She wasn't even really sure she wanted to find love. She had a great job that she enjoyed most of the time. She had great friends, she had a great rental house…she was content with her life for the most part. "Why did I let them talk me into this?" Sam mumbled as they were herded off the stage.

The rest of the morning was torture. All the other contestants were busy talking amongst themselves, already figuring out that Sam didn't fit into "their" crowd. Sam bet they were all rich. They talked about places they'd been to, stores they'd shopped in, and clothing they'd brought with them…all of which meant nothing to Sam.

Later that night, lying in the hotel room, Sam

thought about what her game-plan was going to be. She knew she'd be one of the first people kicked off the show. After all, who would choose her over the other women? She wasn't as pretty, didn't have any fashion sense, was heavier than all of them, and most of all she didn't *want* fame as most of the others seemed to crave. She thought about some of the women she'd met that day. Missy and Katie had hit it off right away, formed their own clique, probably because they were from the "big" cities, LA and New York. Kiki and Courtnee had also paired up, probably because they were both from Florida.

"Wait a minute," Sam said out loud to the empty room. She sat up and started writing down as many names of the other women as she could remember…Brandi, Katie, Cindee, Candi, Amy, Kathi—even her own "name," Sammi. Sam groaned out loud. It couldn't be…it was beyond cheesy, beyond anything she could imagine…all of their names ended with the "ie" sound. Wendi, Nikki, Missy…it was going to be too embarrassing to be on this show. For the millionth time that day she cursed Beth and Christina for getting her into this.

Chapter Three

Alexander David Sanders III watched the closed circuit television in his room intently. He wasn't quite sure how he'd gotten into this situation. Last year he was approached in a local bar and asked if he would pose for a picture for a production company who was looking for reality show contestants. He wasn't interested in doing anything remotely like that, but since he was with Craig and Pete and they egged him into it, he posed. Apparently, they liked his picture and called him in for a round of interviews. He only went to the interviews because Craig and Pete dared him to do it and assured him he'd never get chosen. Two more rounds of interviews after that he'd made the cut and he was chosen. He wasn't really sure what he was chosen for until they flew him out here to Australia. *A freakin' dating show.* Alex thought to himself. He'd never live it down. He liked women—hell, he dated more than his fair share of ladies back in Austin. He never had to worry about finding a date on a Friday or Saturday night for that matter. He wasn't sure how he made it to where he was now, but he didn't have any choice…he was locked into the contract and he had to go through with it.

Alex was told there would be sixteen women who he'd be choosing from. Some weeks he'd be deciding who would go home, and other weeks the ladies themselves would choose. The producer also told him that other weeks there would be a competition and the "loser" would leave. At the end of the show, there'd be one lady left and that was supposed to be his "girlfriend" and hopefully future spouse. It was utterly ridiculous. How was he supposed to get to know sixteen women enough to know who they really were in a few weeks? He'd watched enough dating reality shows to know the women acted very differently to each other than to the "bachelor." He knew some would only be there to be on TV. He wasn't sure he even *wanted* to find a girlfriend. He knew the producers were going to tell the women that he was a rich cowboy who owned a huge spread of land back in Texas, which wasn't quite true. Yes, he did own his own piece of land and had a few cows and horses, but it definitely wasn't a "huge spread" and he definitely wasn't rich. He wasn't hurting for money, true, but it wasn't like he was a millionaire or anything.

Thinking back to the concept of finding a girlfriend on a reality show, he *was* a busy man and he sure hadn't been able to find someone to love back home, so maybe he should give this reality show thing a chance. He figured that if it didn't work out, he'd have a great vacation in Australia, spend some time with beautiful women and maybe drum up some business for himself when it was all said and done.

So here he was, in the Outback, in a hotel room, watching closed circuit television. When he arrived in Australia a few days ago Eddie and the other producers sat him down and explained how the show would work. This show would be a bit different than others because he'd have 24/7 access to any of the tapes of the women or locations that he wanted. He'd see what the contestants did when they weren't around him. He could see their "true nature" when they were around the other contestants. He could see what they looked like without makeup on, he could see how they interacted, and most importantly, he could hear what they said about him when they weren't around him. When he heard that, he became almost excited about this adventure he was about to go on. He knew how to manipulate people with the best of them, and it was going to be great to see how, and if, these women tried to manipulate him.

So he was in his room, watching the "get to know you" function that the contestants were required to attend. It was his first chance to see the contestants before they met him. He kept his fingers crossed that they'd be beautiful. He'd seen that one reality show where the "bachelorette" was introduced to the contestants and they were all unattractive nerds. He wasn't a snob, but he didn't know if he could handle that, even with a signed contract.

At first the room was pretty empty. There were a few people milling around. Once the room started filling up he could pretty much guess which women were the contestants and which were a part of the crew. There were redheads, blondes, brunettes and even one woman with long, straight black hair. Alex relaxed a bit. Thank God, they were beautiful! He watched as Eddie got up on stage and started introducing the women one by one.

"Katie from New York City, Brandi from Phoenix, Kimmie from San Diego, Ashley from Toledo, Cindee from Albany, Lori from Colorado Springs, KiKi from Miami, Courtnee from Pensacola…"

The women all lined up on the stage. Alex

15

chuckled as it reminded him of the "Miss America" pageant he'd been forced to watch when he was younger.

"Candi from Greensboro, Jennie from Billings, Missy from Los Angeles, Sammi from Albuquerque…"

Alex sat forward in his chair and leaned in closer to the screen. That last woman…Sammi…she didn't look like the other contestants. For one, he hadn't noticed her earlier when he'd been watching everyone mingle. He wondered where she'd been. She was also dressed much differently than everyone else. She had on a pair of jeans. They weren't torn or ratty, but looked well-worn and comfortable…something that she didn't look like. If Alex was not mistaken, it looked like she was blushing. It was hard to tell from the little screen he was looking at and the distance the camera was from her, but it was definitely surprising. The producer was continuing the introductions…

"Wendi from Las Vegas, Nikki from Seattle, Amy from El Paso, and last but not least Kathi from Knoxville. Remember these faces, everyone, these are our new contestants for our show called "Love in the Outback."

Alex groaned. *Man, that name sucks.* Hopefully he could talk to them and get them to change it. Alex watched the women walk off the stage. His eyes kept going to the woman in the jeans. He bet she felt self-conscious and out of place. He couldn't remember her name, but because of her differences she'd caught his eye. It was definitely going to be an interesting few weeks.

Chapter Four

The next morning Sam went downstairs with her two bags to gather before meeting their transportation. The other women slowly started entering the ballroom they were to wait in. Most were dragging their bags and they all had at least two full sized suitcases, plus numerous other small handbags.

I hope we do end up camping, Sam thought to herself viciously, it would serve them right if they had to haul their bags all over the Outback.

Eddie came into the room and gleefully announced, "Okay, everyone, our transportation is here, but there's room for only one bag for each of you, plus one carry on. You'll need to go through your belongings and make sure you only bring the essentials that can fit into one suitcase. You have ten minutes before we'll be leaving."

The look on everyone's face was priceless. Panic, sheer terror moved through the women like a stadium full of fans doing the wave. Sam watched as the women flung their bags down and started throwing their clothes out and around them, searching through for what they thought they *had* to have.

"Should I bring my silk camisole?" Candi asked no one and everyone as she shuffled through her clothes.

"I *have* to bring my hair dryer and curling iron," Wendi shrieked as she tried to stuff more and more of her belongings into one suitcase that was already full to the brim.

17

"This isn't fair!" wailed Kimmie. "Why didn't they tell us this last night?!?"

Sam was leaning against the wall, enjoying the discomfort of everyone when Missy looked up and noticed that she wasn't unpacking.

"What's wrong with you, Miss Bitch?" she asked nastily, getting the attention of most of the other women in the room. "You only brought one suitcase to begin with? What, can't you afford designer clothes? Probably not since you wore those horrible jeans last night and have them on again today. Are we going to have to look at you in the same clothes every day until you are kicked off? Hopefully you brought clean underwear!"

With that she started to laugh hysterically at her own joke. Her laugh was loud and braying. Sam looked around and saw most of the other girls were either laughing outright or at least smirking as they continued to rifle through their own belongings. Sam finally answered Missy.

"I figured that since we were going to the Outback we'd probably not have the opportunities to wear much Gucci or Prada, but if we do, I'm sure you'll point out my deficiencies." Somehow Sam made it sound offhand and flippant, when inside she was hoping that the first person would be kicked off before the bus left, and that it'd be Missy.

Eddie came back into the room in exactly ten minutes and started trying to herd everyone out of the room. It looked like a disaster area. There were clothes everywhere. Some of the women were still trying to close their suitcases, which were bulging at the seams with way too many clothes. The random TV employees had to help zip up and close suitcases before they were herded out to a large bus. Sam chuckled. She knew many of the other women were hoping they'd be brought to the place they'd be staying at in stretch limousines. Or maybe like the other reality show that was set in the Outback they'd be skydiving to their destination. But a bus…how plain, how…normal!

Sam had overheard the women speculating the night before about what the house they would be living in would look like. In most of the other reality shows she'd seen the house was beautiful. There were always tons of bedrooms that looked like they were sets for a magazine. There were usually fish tanks and a professional chef-kitchen as well. Sam hoped they wouldn't all be in the same room. She could barely tolerate most of the women for the time the introductions took place last night, there was no way she's be able to handle living with all of them 24/7!

With their bags stowed under the bus everyone took their seats. Sam always liked to sit in the front of a bus. She could see where they were going and ever since she'd seen the movie *Speed* she imagined that if the driver was ever killed or injured, she could heroically take over and save the day. Silly, but she was a romantic at heart. She'd watched that movie a hundred times. When Keanu and Sandra had slid out of the bus together, lain in the dirt and stared into each others' eyes…whew…that was her favorite part. Sam looked at the driver. She couldn't really tell what he looked like. While he wasn't fat, he wasn't a Keanu Reeves either. When the signal was given by a woman standing outside, the bus driver started up the bus and

19

drove off. The producer wasn't onboard with them, but there was a woman with a camera. The show had started.

* * *

Sam was dozing off when she heard "Hey, Sammi."

She looked over to her left and one of the women...Lori from Colorado Springs, Sam thought, was talking to her.

"Hey, Sammi, where do you think we're going? When do you think we'll get to meet the guy?" At least one of the women was being friendly. Sam was starting to think she'd be a total outcast.

"Um, I'm not sure. I think these shows are all about making us try to guess stuff. As for when we'll meet the guy, we'll probably meet him before we know we are meeting him. These reality shows love to give the guy a sneak peak of his pickings." Sam laughed at herself and then couldn't stop herself from saying next, "Do we know that we're competing for a *man*? Maybe it's a woman."

Lori looked horrified, obviously that hadn't occurred to her.

"I'm just kidding, Lori. I'm sure it'll be a guy." Sam had to remind herself to try to rein in her sarcasm. Not everyone appreciated it, and she didn't think the other women would be like Beth and Christina and join in.

Lori looked relieved that Sam thought they'd be meeting a guy and nodded her head, then said, "You're probably right about when we get to meet him. I'd better make sure I look all right then, never know when he'll pop in".

Lori proceeded to take out a small pocket mirror and repair her already perfect makeup. *At least she was semi-friendly,* Sam thought to herself, *even if a little self-absorbed.*

Alex tried to control his smirk. Driving the bus wasn't hard. Not that he'd ever done it before, but he was given a short and fast lesson the night before. He was to drive the women to their lodging. He was able to watch all the women climb on the bus and overhear their conversations. Most were complaining about the fact that they had to leave some of their shoes and fancy dresses behind. Others were complaining about having to travel by bus. He knew they expected something fancier. Some of the women didn't say anything as they climbed on board.

Once again he noticed that the woman called Sammi stood out like a beacon of light in the darkness. She wasn't wearing designer clothes and he didn't think she was even wearing makeup. She certainly wasn't beautiful, now that he could see her close up, but she wasn't a troll either. She didn't flaunt her body as some of the other women did. In fact, it was hard to tell what she looked like under the baggy T-shirt she was wearing.

Since Sammi and Lori were sitting in the seats closest to the driver, Alex could overhear their conversation easily. He almost broke his cover when he heard Sammi's comment about him maybe being a woman. He changed his laugh to a cough at the last second. He wasn't above using sarcasm on occasion and it was refreshing to hear someone being real.

Sammi did have the producers pegged, though. She'd obviously seen enough reality shows to know some of the tricks. But he thought that even she'd be surprised to learn that he was the "guy" they would meet later that night. He wondered if any of the other women had any idea about what was in store for them. He would bet Sammi had some ideas.

They'd been on the bus for a couple of hours when it pulled up to a desolate area. Alex heard one of the women say, "Oh no, please tell me they aren't going to dump us here in the middle of nowhere!" Eddie, who'd been following the bus in an air conditioned limo, climbed aboard and announced that each woman was going to do an introductory video for the "bachelor." The order in which the videos were taped was the order the "bachelor" was going to watch them.

Before he could continue, Jennie called out, "I want to be first!" And just like that pandemonium erupted.

There were shouts of "No Fair!" and "I want to be last" and "That's dumb!" Finally Eddie quieted everyone down and explained that the order the bachelor would watch the videos would be determined by the women themselves. They had to work together and come up with a way to figure out who would speak first, second and so forth. They had twenty minutes to work it out.

Sam heard Eddie chuckling as he left the bus. Missy immediately stood up and said, "Okay, everyone, we need someone in charge and I think I'm the best person." Sam rolled her eyes as Missy continued. "So I want everyone who wants to be first to go to the front of the bus. Everyone who wants to be last go to the back of the bus. If someone doesn't care, go to the middle of the bus".

Sam thought it was actually a good way to at least start the process. After all, they only had twenty minutes to decide. Sam went to the middle of the bus. She honestly didn't care. She didn't think the guy would even notice her with all the other women. There were two women who came to the middle of the bus with her. Amy and Nikki also claimed they didn't care where they went in the video introductions. There were eight women who wanted to be first and another five who wanted to be last. They figured they'd have the best chance to be remembered by the bachelor.

The bickering continued. Sam just sat in the middle and halfway listened to both sides of the bus. She glanced up at one point and found the driver intently staring into the mirror over his head. Sam chuckled to herself. *Must be quite a sight to see all these beauties with their claws out.* It seemed as if the back of the bus had figured out their order, but the front was still pretty heated about whether Missy or Jennie was going to be first. Eddie came back on board and told everyone to get off and to line up in the order of who was going where. Sam, Amy and Nikki didn't know where they were going, so they just got in the middle of each group and figured it was good enough. Missy finally got her way and stood at the front of the line with a smirk. The producer told them they were going to get back on the bus and do the videos one at a time with the camera lady.

Sam waited patiently for her turn. She squatted down in the shade of the bus and closed her eyes. It was a bit warm outside—a lot warm if you listened to the other women—but it was very peaceful, which was something that Sam wasn't used to. Finally it was Sam's turn. She'd heard all about the things the other women said in their video. They'd bragged about how they knew they were going to catch the guy's attention with their videos. Sam still had no idea what she was going to say. She'd thought about it the entire time she was waiting for her turn, but still wasn't sure what she was going to say. As she stepped on the bus she saw the bus driver slumped in his seat with his hat pulled down over his eyes. It looked like he was sleeping soundly. *Those other videos must not have been that exciting.* Sam chuckled.

Sam sat down on the seat as the camerawoman settled across from her. "I'm not really sure where to start," Sam said to the camerawoman, whose name she learned was Kina.

"Just introduce yourself and try to tell the bachelor what makes you special," Kina responded. Sam took a deep breath and when she saw the red light on the camera started.

"Hi. My name is Sammi and I live in Albuquerque, New Mexico. I'm not sure what I'm really supposed to say here, it's like a blind date…really blind on my part since I have no idea who you are." Sammi shifted uncomfortably in her seat and cleared her throat as she continued.

"I'm not sure what you'd want to know about me. I'm thirty-three years old and I rent a small house in the Four Hills area of Albuquerque…oh…I forgot…you probably don't know where that is. It's on the east side of the city near the Interstate. Um, I love animals, especially dogs…in fact, I have three…two basset hounds and a Bloodhound. They're all rescues, I got the bassets from Arizona Basset Hound Rescue and their names are Blue and Albert, and the Bloodhound I got from the local shelter and his name is Duke…um…I'm not sure what else interesting there is about me…I'm not allowed to talk about what I do for a living, so um…"

Sam looked around the bus for some inspiration as to what she should say next. Of course, all she saw was the bus seats and the driver, who looked like he was snoring in the front seat.

"Um…so I like to sit in the front seat of the bus…I usually won't ever sit more than the second seat back from the front and it's all because of the movie *Speed*. It had Sandra Bullock in it…anyway, so in the movie Sandra's character saved the day when she took over driving the bus when the driver was wounded. I've always thought that would be something I could do, so just in case I sit near the front so I can take over…"

Sam paused, then looked at Kina and asked, "Can I say cut?"

Kina looked up from the viewfinder, cut the camera and said, "What's up?"

"Okay, I know this is supposed to be "reality" TV and be live and all of that, but that story just made me sound like the biggest dork in the world…can we please rewind that and let me say something else? I'd just die if the guy heard that."

Kina chuckled and said, "Sure, some of the others wanted to re-do their bits too, not a big deal."

Sam sighed with relief and said more to herself than to Kina, "Okay, now I just have to figure out what

I do want to say."

Kina lifted the camera back up and the red light came back on. Show time.

"Okay, so you know where I live and that I live with three fur kids…I guess one question that sometimes gets asked in awkward moments when people don't know what to say to someone is 'what would you do if you won the lottery?' Let's see…I'd most likely quit my job, I'd tell you what I do, but then the producer would have to kill me." Sam chuckled at herself and then continued, "But I'd want to do something. There's no way that I could just sit at home every day. I'd go stir crazy. I would probably donate money or put money in a trust of some sort for some of the rescue groups that help animals and dogs. There are so many unwanted dogs and the rescue groups do so much with so little. It'd be nice to be able to spread that wealth around a bit and be able to help more animals." Sam laughed. "I probably sound like a do-gooder, but it's not my fault…you try thinking of something interesting to tell someone you've never met! I hope you have a good time with this show, and that you meet someone you could consider spending the rest of your life with. I'm actually looking forward to meeting you."

Sam looked into the camera expectantly. Kina turned it off and lowered the large lens. "All done?" she asked.

"Yup, I suppose that's as good as it's going to be," Sam responded, blushing. "Just promise that you'll edit that before it gets shown on National TV!" Kina laughed, as Sam wanted her to, and she got up and stepped off the bus. After she left Kina met Alex's eyes, which were now open and looking in the mirror over the driver's seat again.

"That was interesting," Kina said. "Much different than the other ones."

Alex agreed, she not only looked different, but she was a breath of fresh air. Most of the other women talked about how they liked to shop and where they liked to eat, and all of the important people they knew. Some almost stripped off their tops and showed off their cleavage throughout the video. And that story about the bus…Alex knew Sammi would be mortified to know that he was the "guy" and that he'd heard that story. He'd already heard a short version of it when she was talking to Lori in the front seats, but hearing it again made her seem a bit more "human" and down to earth. Everyone had fantasies and in a small way she was ready to fulfill that. Alex sighed…not too many more of these videos to sit through and they would be on their way.

After a couple of hours, and after each of the women got to record their introduction, they were finally on their way again. Sam had a headache. Listening to the other women was exhausting and irritating. They asked the same questions over and over and had the same complaints. It was too hot, when would they get there, where were they going, when were they going to meet the bachelor…why couldn't they just go-with-the-flow? The producers would bring forth the guy when they were darn good and ready and not one second earlier. Finally, they pulled up to what looked like would have been an old Girl Scout or Boy Scout camp if they were in the U.S. There were a few trees and what looked like a fire circle and three small buildings.

They all filed off the bus toward the buildings. The two outer buildings were large open rooms that were filled with bunk beds. Obviously they'd reached the end of the bus ride. This was where they'd be staying. The other smaller building was the toilets. There were two toilet pits with two small sinks. There was also one shower head that looked like it had seen better days.

There wasn't a lot being said by the other women. It was obvious this was not what they expected or wanted. Sam just laughed inside. It was perfect. It was what she'd somewhat expected and it was hilarious now that she'd met the other contestants. The sound of the bus starting up and driving away had all the women turning toward where the bus once stood. All of the luggage was sitting on the side of the road. It looked like it had been abandoned, except for the fact that most of it was designer brands. The women went and collected their bags, then started to drag them toward the bunks. There was some discussion about who would sleep where, but most of the women were tired, hot and cranky, not caring much at the moment about where they'd sleep.

Alex drove the bus about five miles down the road to where the main camp for the show was set up. Since he'd would be allowed to see any footage of the women that he wanted, the show decided they might as well save some money and let him stay in the main camp. It was a bit better than where the contestants were staying, but the bunk beds were still in evidence. Alex was allowed his own small tent a bit off to the side of the rest of the production company.

Alex went to his room and lay down on his bed to think about the first day. The women were everything he could have hoped for. They were beautiful, slender, easy on the eyes, but after listening to them talk to each other and having to listen to their boring conversations all day, he was ready to turn his back on the entire project. What did the people that cast this show do? Give an IQ test and only choose women who scored low? Sure they were all great looking, but he'd reached a point in his life where he wanted more. He wasn't sure he was ready to settle down and get married yet, but he also needed more than a pretty face, he wanted intelligent conversation as well. Not all of the women were horrible, he conceded, but man, this was going to be a tough road.

While he remembered the crazy videos, his mind went back to Sammi. He didn't even know her, but her face kept coming to his mind. She had a funny sense of humor and a crooked smile. Alex had never believed in love at first sight, and he still didn't think he did, but there was just something about her that he couldn't put out of his mind.

Suddenly, Eddie knocked on his door and walked in. "What'd ya think, Alex?" he boomed. "Quite a field to choose from, huh?"

"Uh yeah, they certainly are interesting," Alex mumbled.

"Here's the thing," Eddie said with a slimy smirk on his face. "We're going to start off the day tomorrow by kicking one of them off."

"Already?!?" Alex exclaimed. "I haven't even met them officially yet!"

"We know." Eddie cackled. "We're going to

pretend that it's a random thing, but we want you to choose tonight who you want gone. You're going to have most of the choices throughout this process, even if the women don't know it, so think about it and let me know in about an hour who it's gonna be so we can set it all up." And with that he was gone.

How am I going to choose? Thought Alex. He didn't really know these women, and he was supposed to get rid of one already? But then he knew. He'd sat through the video and couldn't believe that she was saying the things that she was and that she'd practically invited herself to move in with him after the show was over. She'd also insulted and belittled some of the other contestants in her video as well. He didn't think he could even pretend to like her when he met her for real. Wendi had to go. Alex figured that maybe it was because she was from Vegas, it was a cutthroat kind of town, and Alex had no desire to even go down that road. When the producer came back about an hour later, Alex told him his choice and the producer left.

Tomorrow would definitely be an interesting day for everyone.

Chapter Five

The next morning was interesting. There were sixteen women trying to cram into the small bathroom building, all trying to use the mirror to do their hair and makeup, not to mention the rush for the shower…until they found out there wasn't any hot water. Most of the women decided they didn't need a shower after all. Sam found the entire situation pretty amusing. Since the shower wasn't being used because there wasn't any hot water, Sam took a quick dunk and washed her hair. She then went back to her bunk, got dressed, brushed her hair, twisted it up into a barrette, and she was ready to face the day. It took her about half an hour to get ready, so she was ready quite a bit ahead of the others. She decided she'd explore a little around the campsite before things got started. The cameramen and women were busy filming the women who were still trying to get ready and didn't notice when Sam slipped out of the camp.

Sam observed that their camp seemed to be at the bottom of a slight rise. She started walking up the hill to see what was on the other side. When she got to the top she just stopped and stared…it was beautiful. It'd be the kind of place she'd love to build a house. She was staring out at the Outback. She couldn't believe she was actually here. The sun had already come up and everything had a slight orange tint to it. There were rolling hills, trees, open spaces that looked like desert, and there was even a creek or river or something in the distance. The sounds of animals were loud. She had no idea what animals were making the sounds, but it was beautiful. Sam sat down on a nearby rock. What an unbelievable sight. If nothing else, she was glad she'd been chosen for this silly show just so she could see this. Sam sat there just drinking in the sight of the land in front of her for a while, when suddenly she heard a commotion back at camp. She reluctantly rose and started back down the hill. It looked like this show would be getting started today after all.

When she arrived back at the camp the other women were running around franticly. Eddie was there. Courtnee told Sam as she ran past that they had five minutes to meet at the flat open space near the fire circle. Finally all the women were lined up in two rows around the "host" of the show. This was a man they hadn't met before. His name, they were told, was Robert. He was tall and good-looking in a movie star way. He didn't interact with the other women in any way until the camera turned on him and Eddie said "roll." Suddenly, his entire face lit up in a wide smile.

"Welcome, ladies. I'm Robert. I'll be your host for this dating journey you're about to embark on. Later today you will meet the bachelor and I'm sure you will be impressed and excited." Robert paused dramatically, then continued, "But first there is one piece of business we have to attend to. As you know, at random times during the next few weeks one of you will be leaving the show." Some of the women let out disappointed moans as if on cue.

"I know, I know," Robert continued, "but it can't be helped. In fact, one of you will be going home today, right now as a matter of fact."

There were shocked gasps from the group of women. Comments like "No way!" and "I can't believe it" and "That isn't fair" and "We haven't even met the bachelor yet!" were heard.

Sam couldn't help it. She laughed out loud and got quite a few glares from the other women.

"I know you're wondering how this will be done since you haven't even met the bachelor yet. Since we want this game to be as fair as possible and since most of you don't even know each other yet, we are going to draw names out of a hat. If your name is drawn, you're safe, if your name is the last one left, then you'll be going back home."

It's perfect, Sam thought, *totally random and objective.* She wondered if this would be her last day in the Outback. She didn't really care about the guy, after all she hadn't even met him yet, but it was such a beautiful place, it would be a shame not to get to see more than this little campsite, especially after her time on the rise. Another part of her, a part she wouldn't admit to if asked, wanted to see the guy. She figured that all women had a fantasy of being chosen above others, and she was no exception. She shook herself and forced herself to pay attention.

"Okay," Robert continued, "Here's the hat. I'd like for each of you to come forward and take your name and place it into the hat." The hat was a big ten gallon cowboy hat. The names were elaborate name plates that were the kind of thing that would sit on someone's desk at work. They were black plastic with big white letters.

What a cheesy prop. Sam thought as she got in line to grab her nameplate and put it in the hat. *I guess*

I won't be crumpling up my piece of paper. She placed her name in with the others. Sam had a trick she used in various raffles that she'd participated in. She knew that if you crumpled up your ticket, it was more likely to be chosen because it would feel different than the others in the mix. There was no possibility of these plastic pieces being crumpled, though, darn it.

Slowly, Robert started calling out names.

"Katie, Nikki, Kimmie, Cindee…" After each name was called the camera zoomed in on the woman as she stepped away from the others to a separate platform. Robert continued, "Lori, Kiki, Courtnee, Kathi, Missy, Candi…" Sam saw Candi actually tearing up as she stepped to the new platform. *Give me a break.* Sam thought. *She doesn't even* know *the guy yet!* Five more names to be called. Sam started to get a bit nervous. She really didn't want to be the first person to leave the show. It was too much like getting picked last at kickball when she was in elementary school. She didn't want to be the first loser. "Amy, Brandi…" Sam held her breath. "Sammi…" *Thank God.* Sam thought as she took her place on the other platform.

There were now only three women left on the other platform. All three looked like they were going to cry.

"Ashley," Robert called as he pulled one more piece of paper from the hat. Ashley squealed and ran over to the other platform and hugged Candi. Sam inwardly rolled her eyes at their antics. The only two women who were left were Wendi and Jennie. Sam couldn't help but feel a bit sorry for them. It certainly wouldn't be any fun to be in their situation. Finally, after making a dramatic speech, Robert pulled the last name out of the hat.

"Jennie." Wendi would be the first contestant to be leaving the show. Wendi didn't say a word. She just turned around and walked toward the bunk. Robert didn't look like he knew what he was supposed to do in response. Sam figured they were probably supposed to all go over and console Wendi and it was supposed to be a bit cry fest. *Whatever.*

Eddie and the TV other staff assisted Wendi in packing her belongings and she was whisked out of the campsite fairly rapidly. The women weren't sure what they were supposed to be doing next when the producer asked them all to climb back on the bus. They all trudged back to the bus they'd ridden in yesterday like good little contestants. Sam, once again, claimed the front seat. She absently noticed that today's driver was a different man than the one who'd driven them to the camp the day before. He wasn't nearly as buff as the first driver. Sam shook her head at herself. Really. Now she was lusting after the bus driver? She needed to get a life!

They were driven to an area next to a small river. It wasn't too far across, maybe about twelve feet. Sam wasn't sure how deep it was as it was a bit hard to tell. When they got off the bus Robert was once again standing around. He'd ridden in a separate car and was getting his face makeup touched up. *So much for reality.* Sam thought snidely.

The women were instructed to stand in their two lines again on a portable podium that was set up for them. Once they were all in place Robert stepped up to his place in front of the podium and started to speak.

"Today is the day that you'll meet our bachelor. He's looking forward to getting to know you all. He's watched all of your videos and is anxious to meet you. Instead of having a large meet and greet, as is normal for shows like this, today we are going to have a contest." Most of the women groaned. "*Some* of you will get to meet him today. The others will have to wait until another day. I'm sure you all know how important it is to get to know the bachelor since in the future he'll be deciding who stays and who goes."

The women immediately started talking to each other. Robert allowed this for a while as it was a good dramatic effect to his announcement.

That's sneaky. Sam thought to herself. *Make us compete against each other to see who'll get to meet him first and make an impression.* Sam decided there was no way she was going to get into a pissing match with the other women. There would be plenty of time for her to meet the guy and she wasn't going to get caught in the middle of any catfight. That had never been her style and it wasn't going to change now.

Robert continued his speech, "Each of you will have ten minutes to follow the path," Robert said as he pointed to a path that continued along the river. "At the end of the path there's a large barrel filled with water. You have to reach in and grab one fish, then bring it back down the path and place it into your pail here. Since there are fifteen of you, we will run in heats of three people in each heat. There is only one barrel and only twenty fish in the barrel. The eight women that collect the most fish will get to meet the bachelor today. The rest of you will go back to the camp and meet him at a later time."

Complete silence greeted Robert at the end of his speech. But then the women started talking amongst themselves, trying to come up with the best strategy. *This is so corny, but it ought to be funny to watch these women run in their heels!*

The heats were announced. First up would be Kathi, Nikki, and Missy. Heat Two would be Candi, Kiki, and Cindee. Heat Three would be Kimmie, Katie, and Amy. Heat Four would be Sammi, Jennie, and Courtnee, and the last heat would be Lori, Ashley, and Brandi.

Eddie and other TV employees quickly got the first heat ready to go. The course was already set up so it wasn't long before Kathi, Nikki, and Missy were off and running along the path. Since the other contestants couldn't see what was going on at the barrel it was a surprise to see Missy coming running back with a fish…and soaking wet! It looked like she'd dived headfirst into the barrel. The other women giggled uneasily, knowing their turn would come in the not too distant future. Not far behind her was Nikki. The race continued. Missy was obviously determined to get the most fish. Final total at the end of the ten minutes was Missy with eleven fish, Nikki with six and Kathi with only three.

Heat two and three were much of the same. Candi, Katie, and Kiki had eight fish each. Cindee had four, Kimmie and Amy each had six. During heat three Kimmie and Amy were both racing back to their buckets with their last fish and time was quickly winding down when Kimmie slipped on the path and almost fell into the river. Her fish went flying over the path and Kimmie went sprawling after it. She was fine, and she was able to get up and deposit her fish in her bucket before time was up, but it was a sobering moment for everyone. She could have really gotten hurt. The path did look slippery and it didn't look inconceivable that someone could come around the corner and slip and fall into the river. It wouldn't be deadly, the river didn't look that deep and there weren't many rocks around the side of the river, but it certainly wouldn't be a pleasant fall.

It was heat four's turn. Sam, Jennie, and Courtnee were racing down the path toward the bucket. Sam suddenly understood why the women were all wet when they came back with their fish. The bucket was filled to the rim with water and was about three and a half feet tall. In order to reach the fish that were "camped out" at the bottom, you had to lean all the way in and put your head under the water in order to reach the fish. Jennie was the first to arrive at the bucket. She soon had her first fish and was heading back to the pail to deposit it. Courtnee was next and she soon came up with her first fish and was off and running. Sam was in no hurry to get her fish and head back. She stood there, looking down at the fish in the barrel. It was actually kinda sad. She knew that fish were killed every day, but this was different, these fish weren't going to be eaten, they were being killed for a stupid TV show. Slowly, Sam reached in and grabbed one of the fish. It was surprisingly heavy. She heard Jennie running back up the path for her second fish. Sam headed down the path toward her pail. She didn't want it to look like she was deliberately not trying to win, but this was ridiculous. She put her fish in the pail. Then she picked up the pail and walked toward the river. She bent down and filled it with water, then carried it back to the clearing. If she was going to have to collect these fish she was going to keep them alive until the ten minutes were over and then she was going to set them free into the river again.

After about eight minutes most of the fish had been collected. Jennie and Courtnee were neck and neck in the fish department. There were two fish left in the barrel. Sam retrieved one of those two fish and was headed back down the path toward her pail when Jennie and Courtnee came running up the path. They were both determined that they were going to get that last fish. Whoever got that last fish would be the heat winner with eight. As it happened, Sam, Courtnee and Jennie reached the bend in the path at the same time. Sam couldn't move out of the way fast enough and when Jennie brushed past her on her way to the barrel Sam lost her balance and slipped down that same slope that Kimmie almost went down. But this time, Sam went sliding into the river.

It's cold, was Sam's first thought as she went under. The water wasn't very deep, maybe about four and a half feet, but it was freezing. Sam looked up at the path and saw Kina pointing her camera down at her. *Great, just great, I know this is going to make the show.* Since the fish she'd been carrying was long gone, Sam looked up at the bank and tried once to climb up. She figured out pretty quickly that she wasn't going to be able to get back up to the path the way she'd come. It was pretty steep and covered with mud and rocks. She knew there were rocks under the mud because she could feel her side throbbing. She'd obviously scraped herself on those rocks on her way down. In order to get out of the river she'd have to go upstream and see if she could make her way back to the clearing and climb out that way. She heard Jennie and Courtnee go running back down the path. It sounded like Jennie had retrieved that last fish as Courtnee was bitching that Jennie had cheated. They didn't even notice her as they were concentrating on the sound of Robert's voice counting down the time.

With Kina still filming, Sam started making her way back upstream. It was slow going since she slipped on hidden rocks every few feet. Sam was really starting to get cold. She wished she could ask Kina for help, but she knew the rules…she had to pretend the cameras didn't exist. Finally, she made her way to the clearing where everyone turned to stare at her.

"What are you doing?" Brandi asked incredulously.

"I thought I'd take a swim," Sam replied sarcastically while climbing out, dripping water all the way up the bank. When no one said anything else, Sam finally said, "I slipped." She then turned to Robert and asked, "Are all my fish counted?" When Robert answered affirmatively, she walked to her bucket, picked it up and walked back to the stream.

"What are you doing now?" Brandi asked again.

"What does it look like?" Sam responded with a bite to her tone. "My fish are counted, there's no need to let them die needlessly." And with that she emptied the pail into the river and watched her four fish swim away.

The last heat went off without a hitch. Lori and Brandi each retrieved eight fish and Ashley got four. The women who'd get to meet the bachelor that day were Missy with eleven fish, Candi, Katie, Kiki, Jennie, Lori, and Brandi, who all had eight fish, and Courtnee who had gotten seven fish. Sam didn't really care. She was cold and wet and she knew she'd scraped her side pretty good on her way down the incline into the river. All she wanted to do was get back to camp and take a shower, even if it was a cold one, then get into clean clothes. But Robert had another surprise up his sleeve.

"Okay, ladies, everyone did a good job in collecting their fish. If the eight of you who retrieved the most fish would come with me, it's time to meet the bachelor." At his statement words of protest rang out.

"No *way*," Missy said. "I'm sopping wet, my makeup is gone and my hair looks horrible. This isn't fair…I want to go and change first." The other ladies agreed. Robert stood and looked at the group of women. They really did look bedraggled. He smirked.

"Okay, you have a choice, the eight of you who collected the fish can either come right now to meet the bachelor, or you can go back to the camp and meet him first thing in the morning. If you choose to meet him in the morning, the other seven women will go right now and meet him. It's up to you."

Sam just laughed inside. These reality shows really were full of twists and turns. She wasn't sure what decision the winners would make. She knew they really wanted to meet the guy first, but they also wanted to make a good impression and showing up as they were wouldn't do that. But on the other hand they really didn't want anyone *else* to be able to get to him first. It really was going to be a tough choice. Sam

41

hoped they'd let their greediness get the better of them. She really, *really* wanted to go back to camp. It wasn't that she didn't want to meet the guy looking like she did, she was just cold and miserable. And fixing that came before any man. Normally she wouldn't have been so cold, but the sun had disappeared during their little competition, and with the loss of the sun went the loss of much of the heat of the day.

The eight women were huddled together a bit away from the camp. The ever-present Kina hovered as close as she could with the camera. Sam tried to ignore her, she hadn't quite gotten the hang of ignoring the cameras, but she figured by the time this show was over she wouldn't even think twice about them being around. They could all hear a bit of the conversation every now and then, but for the most part they were being pretty quiet all things considered. Finally Missy stood up. Since she retrieved the most fish, she was obviously in charge.

"For the record, we don't think this is fair. We won the competition fair and square and you tricked us," she said loudly. "But we've decided that we'd rather put our best foot forward tomorrow morning and meet the bachelor. The *losers* can meet him now the way they are."

Of course, the last was said with such distain it was impossible to miss. So the eight women climbed back on the bus and were taken back to camp. The seven women that were left standing in the clearing just laughed. They weren't happy at having to meet the bachelor looking like they were either, but they were a little less wet, except for Sam, than the others because they didn't retrieve as many fish from the barrel.

They were instructed to just sit and wait. Next thing they knew there was a team of people setting up a table and mini-work stations. The fish were brought out by a crew of chefs. The chefs immediately started preparing the fish to be cooked. Sam laughed. *We're going to have quite the meal!* It was hard to get excited about it, though, since her jeans were molded to her body with river water, her side hurt from where it was scraped and she was so cold. She was glad that the fish would be eaten—she assumed they would be cooking the fish from the contest—and not just die for the sake of the contest and the show.

The women sat together and watched the meal being prepared. They tried to finger comb their hair back into some semblance of a hairstyle. Because of the dry air their hair was mostly dry when they heard from behind them, "Hello, ladies".

It was the guy!!!

Susan Stoker

Chapter Six

They all abruptly stood up and turned around. It was time to meet the bachelor. Sam slowly stood up and faced the man she'd been calling "the guy" in her mind. He was tall, about six feet one inch. He was wearing a pair of jeans and a long sleeve collared shirt. He had on cowboy boots and a cowboy hat. Sam couldn't really see the color of his hair, but his eyes were a deep chocolate brown. He had what looked like laugh lines around his eyes.

The ever present Robert spoke then, "Ladies, I would like to introduce you to our bachelor, Al. Al is from Austin, Texas, and owns his own ranching operation outside of the city. He's thirty-eight years old and has never been married. He likes to hunt, fish, camp, and work with animals. He's an expert horseman and I feel confident that he'll keep you safe out here in the wilds of the Outback. I'll leave the eight of you to get acquainted. In four hours I'll return to take you back to camp. Ladies. Al." And with that Robert turned around and left the clearing.

Alex thought it was amusing that first of all they'd shortened his name. Never in his thirty-eight years had anyone ever dared to call him Al. He guessed they wanted to try to preserve some of his privacy when the show finally did air. At least that was what he hoped. He also chuckled at the spin they put on his life. He did like to hunt and do the other things Robert said, and he was an expert horseman, but he knew with the outfit he was wearing it would produce erroneous assumptions about what he did for a living.

Ashley immediately walked over to Al and introduced herself.

"Hi, my name is Ashley. I'm from Toledo, Ohio. It's great to finally meet you. We've been very excited, you're even better looking than I could've imagined. It must be great to own your own ranch!" Alex chuckled to himself. He knew that with that introduction they'd assume he was rich and owned a big ranch.

"Nice to meet you, Ashley," Alex responded neutrally.

One by one the other women lined up to meet Al. They all said where they were from and gushed on and on about how happy they were to meet him. Finally, it was Sam's turn. She held out her hand, shook the guy's hand and simply said "Sammi" by way of introduction. Alex's mouth turned up in the corners.

"That's it?" he asked with a smile.

"Yup," Sam replied. "What ya see is what ya get."

With that Alex took the time to look up and down Sam's body. He noticed that her jeans seemed to be wet, while her hair was dry. He couldn't help but notice her curves. Her jeans were molded to her body, allowing him to see that she was all woman. The blouse she was wearing was also clinging to her body. Sam had her arms crossed defensively in front of her, but that just pushed her breasts up, making them more noticeable. Alex didn't usually ogle women, but damn, this woman had a body that was built to be ogled. His eyes made it back up from his perusal of her body to her face and saw she was blushing. When was the last time he'd seen a woman blush from just a look?

His mind went back to the fact that her jeans were

wet. None of the other women's clothes were clinging to them as hers were. None of the other women seemed to be as soaked as she was. And now that he thought about it, when he shook her hand it was ice cold.

"You seem to be a bit wet," he said with one eyebrow raised up in a question.

"Had a little incident earlier, it was nothing," Sam replied, turned around and went back to sit on a log. She was too embarrassed to get into it. If she hadn't been so clumsy and if she'd paid more attention to what was going on, she wouldn't be in this situation now. She was also embarrassed at the way Al had looked at her. She wasn't an idiot. She knew with her clothes wet, they'd cling to her. She couldn't interpret Al's look, though. She wanted to believe that he was looking at her in a flirty way, but she couldn't fathom it. As was typical for her, when she was embarrassed she retreated into herself and it usually came across as disinterest.

The other women quickly tried to manipulate Alex's conversation. Alex couldn't wait to get back to his tent and watch the tapes of what happened that day. Somehow he just knew there was more to this meeting than the women were letting on. He thought the women all looked nice, he just couldn't put his finger on why they looked different than yesterday when he saw them on the bus. As part of the "meet and greet" Alex was required to spend one-on-one time with all the women. He started with Cindee and then met in quick succession with Amy and Kimmie. They were all pleasant. He didn't have any real positive or negative thoughts about any of them so far.

After speaking with Kimmie it was time to eat.

Sam was starving. It seemed as if shivering used up a
lot of energy and probably calories as well. Fish wasn't
her favorite food, but at the moment she was starving
and would eat anything. The platter of fish was passed
around and everyone took some of the delicious
smelling fish. The chefs had outdone themselves! Sam
was so hungry she just dug right in. She'd taken two
large chunks of fish from the platter. It was quiet for a
bit and slowly conversation started back up. Sam
wasn't interested in what the other women had to say.
It seemed the longer she sat out in the clearing, the
colder and more miserable she got. The lack of sun and
the lateness of the day made the weather cool off
quickly. This was ridiculous. Eddie knew she fell in
the river, why wasn't he helping her get dry clothes?
She knew this was supposed to be a "reality show" but
so far there hadn't been too much reality from her
perspective. She finally looked up and noticed that
everyone else had finished eating. She was the only
one left. Oh well, she was hungry and she wasn't going
to let the meal go to waste. Hell, they'd probably give
them rice and beans to eat back at the camp!

Alex didn't want to be rude and continue his one-
on-one sessions with the women until Sammi had
finished eating. He thought it was unusual that she was
actually eating. It was his experience that most women,
when in the company of a man, just picked at their
food or ate very little. Not Sammi, she'd taken a large
helping of the fish and was eating it with a look of
pleasure on her face. Finally, Sam pushed back her
plate.

"All done," she said with a smile.

One of the chefs came and took her plate. Before

he could back away, Sam touched his sleeve and said quietly, "Thank you, honestly that was the best fish I've ever eaten...and I don't even really like fish!"

The chef laughed and said, "I'll pass the compliment on to the other chefs as well." Then he backed away.

With that Alex knew it was time to finish up the one-on-ones. He talked with Kathi, Ashley, and Nikki, and then it was time to meet with Sammi. He'd been looking forward to talking with her for some reason. He wasn't sure why. She was an odd woman. She didn't seem to fit in any better today with the other women than she did yesterday. She seemed nice enough, but he wasn't sure what to think about it all yet. He looked up as Sammi came around the tree. They were sitting a bit away from the other women in order to give him privacy as he spoke with each lady. Sammi sat down on the log about three feet away from him. Alex was surprised. All the other women practically sat in his lap!

Sam sighed. She knew this was going to come. She didn't really want to be last, but she was tired and cold and didn't feel like fighting the other women for when she would meet with him. She had to be careful, though, because Kina was right there with the camera and she didn't want to look like a pathetic loser on National Television.

"Hello, Al," Sam said.

"Hello, Sammi," Alex replied.

"Good fish, didn't you think?" Sam asked.

"It was great," Alex answered.

God. Sam thought to herself. This was *not* going well. She sounded like a complete dork.

49

"Heh heh, sorry, Al, I don't really know what to say being this is the first time we're really alone." With that she laughed and motioned at the camera a few feet away.

Alex laughed. "Yeah, a bit awkward. Where are you from? You never told me anyway."

"I did tell you," Sam responded.

"No, I distinctly remember you telling me your name and that was about it," Alex said with puzzlement. Where was she going with this?

"I told you in my introduction tape…didn't you watch them?" Sam asked with a smile on her face.

Alex knew that he was caught. She was right. He'd forgotten all about the tapes. He didn't need to watch them, he'd been there.

"You're right, I'd forgotten..." He searched his mind to try to remember where she said that she lived. "Albuquerque, right?"

"Yup, good memory, Al," Sam replied. "I'm surprised you can keep us all straight with our names and all."

"What do you mean?" Alex asked.

"Come on, you can't mean to tell me that you haven't noticed," Sam asked incredulously.

"Noticed what?" Alex asked, honestly confused.

In a sing-song voice Sam answered, "Samm-i, Miss-y, Kath-i, Kimm-ie, Lor-i, Brand-i…get it now?"

Alex threw his head back and laughed until his sides hurt. He'd honestly not even noticed that all of their names ended in the "ie" sound. It was utterly ridiculous.

"I'd thought that perhaps *your* name would be something like Charlie or Bobby," Sammi said with a laugh.

And with that Alex howled with laughter again. "That would be really over the top, huh?" he asked with a grin.

Sam relaxed a bit. It seemed like Al had a pretty good sense of humor after all.

"Come here," Alex said, patting the space next to him.

Sam looked at him with her eyebrows raised and he could see the distrust come over her body. She stiffened and sat up straight on the log. He stifled a sigh, knowing he'd just made her uneasy again and ruined their camaraderie.

"I'm not going to make a pass or cop a feel," he told her gently. "I just feel like I'm shouting at you sitting all the way over there."

Sam slowly scooted over closer to Al. She could feel the warmth emanating off of him, but maybe that was because she was still cold, sitting in damp jeans in the shade. She shivered.

"Are you still cold?" Alex asked, taking her hand in his. "Holy cow, you really are cold, aren't you?" he exclaimed, looking into her face a bit closer.

Sam pulled her hand away from his and said, "I'm fine."

"You're not fine!" Alex said and went to grab her hands back, and in doing so brushed his hand against her leg. "Your jeans are still soaking wet!" he said in shock. "How long have you been walking around with wet clothes on? Tell me it hasn't been the entire time!" he demanded.

"Why do you care?" Sam bit back. "I'm fine. I said I'm fine, I'll change later." And with that she got up and walked back into the clearing. She didn't know why it bothered her so much. Probably because she didn't like to admit to anyone any kind of discomfort or pain. She hated being sick. Always had. Hated relying on others to help her. She was an independent person, one that didn't like to be catered to. When she was little she saw girls all the time faking illnesses or injuries to get sympathy or to get out of doing different jobs. She swore she'd never be like that, and she hadn't. She only went to the doctor when she had to and she never ever liked to admit to anyone that she was in need of help.

But another part of her was angry at herself. She was attracted to Al. He was handsome. He was everything she'd ever dreamed about when she lay in bed at night dreaming about finding someone to spend her life with. She had no idea why she was so ugly to him. There was nothing she wanted more than to snuggle into his arms and have him warm her up. But she wasn't the kind of woman men wanted to snuggle up to. She knew it. Her history had proven that time and time again. She convinced herself that the only reason Al wanted to get close to her was because of the damn show and so he'd look better on camera. She sighed as she walked toward the other women. She was confused and hurting. Al confused her. Her reaction to Al confused her.

"Done already?" Nikki sneered when Sam reentered the clearing.

"Yup," was all Sam could get out.

She felt Al come up behind her. She was tempted to lean back against him for a moment, but common sense prevailed and she ignored him as she headed to sit back on the log with her knees drawn up, her arms looping around them.

The rest of the time seemed to drag by for Sam. She watched as the other women went through a dance with each other of trying to manipulate Al's time and attention. He did his best to try to talk evenly with everyone. Sam noticed every now and then that his eyes would meet hers, but she'd quickly look away, blushing. She didn't feel that she was on an even playing field with him and it made her feel vulnerable, which she hated. He was so obviously out of her league it wasn't funny. He owned his own ranch and was probably richer than she could imagine. Why would he look twice at her when there were all these other beautiful women to choose from? Sam wasn't feeling sorry for herself, she was just being realistic.

Finally, Robert and Eddie came back into the clearing and announced it was time to go. Alex could tell the women wanted to say goodbye individually to him, so he stood a bit away from the group and allowed each of the women to come up, make small talk, say how much they couldn't wait to see him again, and kiss him briefly. Some kissed him on the lips and others kissed him on the cheek. He was amazed that because they were on this show the women felt as if it was okay to kiss him so intimately.

Once again, Sammi was last in line. She walked up to him, held out her hand and quickly, before he could say anything, told him, "Look, I'm sorry about that back there. I'm not having a good day. I know I didn't make a good impression and I'm sorry about that. I'm tired, wet, and yes, cold, and all I want to do is go back and get into some warm clothes. I promise to be on my best behavior the next time we meet." Finally, she looked up and meeting his eyes, she gave him a shy smile. God, he was gorgeous. What she would do to start over with him. Hell, what she would do to have met him in a normal situation and not on this stupid reality show.

Alex grasped Sammi's hand with both of his and tried to infuse some of his warmth into it. "It's okay, I didn't have any right to pry and I was out of line. How about if I promise to only talk about the weather and other non-threatening topics next time?" Alex asked with a smile.

Sam smiled back and said, "Deal."

Alex slowly raised her hand, kissed the back of it and let her go. He watched as she blushed a fiery red and turned away to climb into the bus.

He couldn't help but notice that she had the sexiest back-end he'd ever seen as she stepped up into the bus. She filled out her jeans in all the right ways. He'd never really thought about what "type" of woman he was interested in, but seeing Sammi step up into the bus did something to him. He felt himself get hard as she rounded the corner and sat down in the front seat of the bus. He took a deep breath to try to calm himself down. He'd forgotten about her penchant to sit in the front seat and wished he could tease her later about it, but he wasn't supposed to have seen that part of the tape she'd made. He thought it was interesting that she was the only one who hadn't kissed him. She wasn't even trying to catch his attention, but she had by being herself. He wanted to watch the day's tape more than ever now. He wanted to know what had happened that day to make Sammi's jeans soaking wet.

Chapter Seven

Alex pushed play on the tape that Eddie gave him of that morning's contest. He knew there were several different cameras taping the women at any given time, but the tape he had in his hand was from the camera that had been on the path. He could see most of the competition because of the angle of the camera. He watched as Kathi, Nikki, and Missy raced down the lane. Missy was the first one back on the path. He had to laugh at his first glimpse of the women after their encounter with the barrel. They were dripping from head to toe, looking like bedraggled little kids. Missy raced back and forth and was obviously determined to have the most fish.

The next two heats were much of the same. He could just see the barrel that the women were diving head first into and he could just barely see the clearing where they were putting the fish into pails. The camera was right on the curve in the path. The next heat was Sammi's heat. Alex watched as Jennie, Courtnee, and Sammi raced up the path. He laughed at the look on Jennie's and Courtnee's faces as they raced by. They looked determined, to say the least. Sammi was running, but it seemed to Alex that she wasn't trying very hard. The tapes were actually getting pretty boring just watching the women run back and forth. Most of the way through the fourth heat Alex finally saw why Sammi had been so cold and wet. The camera was focused on Jennie and Courtnee running back up the path. They were jostling each other to get to the barrel first. Alex couldn't see exactly what happened because the camera suddenly pointed toward the sky, but the next thing he saw was Sammi looking up at the camera from the river. He could put together the pieces and he assumed that the two running women had knocked Sammi off the path and into the river.

Sammi was standing in water that was up to around her chest. She was looking up at the camera as if to ask for help, but knew none would be forthcoming. Alex's hands clenched at his side. Damn it, the other two women didn't even stop! Soon he saw Sammi make one attempt to climb up the side of the riverbank only to slide back down again in the mud. She then started to make her way upstream. Every now and then she would look up at the camera. He chuckled at the words that were coming out of her mouth. Oh, she was muttering to herself, but some of what she was saying was loud enough to carry to the camera. Alex heard Jennie and Courtnee run past the camera, screeching as they headed toward the clearing, but they didn't stop to help Sammi. The camera stayed focused on Sammi as she struggled to get upstream and to the clearing. Obviously, the camera operator knew where the real "money shot" was. Alex watched Sammi finally reach the clearing and get to a point where the water was only at her knees. He watched her climb out of the water, go toward one of the pails, grab it and go back to the river only to dump out the fish. He laughed then. She wasn't kidding when she'd told him she liked animals on her video tape.

Alex continued to watch and learned how the "losers" came to be the ones to meet him that day. He thought it was pretty clever of the producers, but he also made a mental note to make sure he didn't underestimate them in any way because he knew they could always turn around and do the same sort of thing to him. What he couldn't believe was that not one person offered Sammi a towel or gave her any sympathy for falling into the river. He would have thought—no, hoped, that at least some of the other women would have been sympathetic enough to care about Sammi and what had happened. Unfortunately, not one of them offered an ear, a hand, or any type of assistance.

The camera operator seemed to know that Sammi was cold because she kept panning in very close to Sammi's chattering teeth and shaking body. Alex sighed. There was nothing he could do. He wasn't even supposed to be watching the tapes for God's sake, but he wasn't the kind of man who usually let a woman suffer, even if it was only something as small as her being chilly.

Alex suddenly had to know if Sammi had managed to warm herself up and if she was all right. He was also curious to see what the other women had talked about when the ladies he met today went back to camp. He knew he'd be meeting them the next day and he wanted to have some idea of what to expect from them. Alex wandered out of his tent and over to the production tent. Eddie was still there and Alex told him, "I'd like to see a tape of what went on when the women got back to camp." Eddie didn't seem to mind and asked one of the editors for the tape.

Alex wasn't sure what to expect when he sat down to watch it. He figured that the other women would be jealous, and he was right. There was a lot of interrogation that went on. The women that he didn't get to meet today asked all sorts of questions about what he looked like, what he was wearing, what he said, if he kissed any of them. Alex was surprised when Nikki claimed they'd kissed during their one-on-one session. He just shook his head. It was definitely going to be interesting to see the dynamics unfold in the ladies' camp.

The fact that he could watch these tapes was probably one of the only reasons he was still on the show. He couldn't image trying to wade through what was real and what was fake if he didn't have the tapes to watch. He counted himself lucky in that sense. The last thing he wanted to do was have feelings toward one of the women and then find out that it was all a lie. Eddie was a sneaky bastard and seemed to know how to push and just how far to go to make good TV.

Alex tried to catch of glimpse of Sammi on the tapes of the camp, but he didn't see her anywhere. He watched as the camera in the bathhouse caught the ladies brushing their teeth over the sinks and washing off their makeup, generally doing what women did to get ready for bed. The cameras didn't show the bathrooms at all, only the sink area, thank God. There was no way he wanted anything to do with any type of "peeping Tom" kind of thing. He still didn't see Sammi anywhere in the group, and he found himself really looking for her.

Finally, the light went off in the bathroom camera. He knew that that camera was hooked up to the light. When the light went on, the camera started taping. Eddie and the other producers had purposely blocked all the natural light from the building so even in the middle of the day the women had to turn the light on if they wanted to see in the small dark building. It was one more sneaky thing that had been orchestrated on the show. Alex knew he should never underestimate them. This camera was also one that Alex didn't think the ladies knew about. If they had, he was sure they'd be playing to it and watching what they said to each other and about him. He sure had gotten an earful about what his butt looked like in his jeans and about their speculation about the size of his package.

He was about to call it a night when the bathroom camera suddenly came on again. The time stamp on the video said that it was about two hours after the other women had left. It was Sammi coming into the bathroom. She looked behind her as she shut the door. It looked like she was trying to see if she'd been followed or if there was a camera anywhere around. Alex found himself leaning toward the small TV, trying to get a better view of the woman. He didn't even try to kid himself and say that he wasn't interested in her. He was.

Sammi was carrying a small case. It looked like a cosmetic bag. Alex watched as Sammi went over to one of the sinks in front of the large mirror. She looked around furtively one more time, and finding no one, took a deep breath and lifted up her T-shirt on her left side. Alex gasped at the same time that Sammi said, "Damn." There were giant scrapes down the entire length of her side. Alex watched as Sammi lowered her shirt and reached into her cosmetic bag. She brought out a tube of something and lifted her shirt again. Because of the camera angle Alex could see everything she was doing. She started to smear what looked like a lotion on her side. Alex sucked in a breath at the same time that Sammi did. It had to hurt. *She must be putting antibiotic cream on it.* Alex thought to himself. Smart, but he was still mad that Eddie knew about this but hadn't done anything. It was ridiculous and dangerous.

Alex watched as Sammi finished spreading the cream on herself and put both her hands on the counter and leaned against them. She closed her eyes, dropped her head and again took a deep breath. Again, Alex's hands clenched into fists. She was in pain, and obviously trying to breathe through it. He wanted nothing more than to take her into his arms and hold her to help her work through that pain. Alex watched as Sammi stood as still as a gazelle in the sights of a hungry lion and remembered what her body looked like. He swallowed hard. He was supposed to be thinking about how hurt she was, but the only thing he could think of was how silky her skin looked. He thought about how Sammi was all woman. She wasn't stick thin, he couldn't see her ribs, but he knew she'd be soft, and he'd be able to hold on to her and feel the give in her body, as a woman should feel. He finally shook his head and willed Sammi to feel better.

Finally, he saw her take one last deep breath and look up at the mirror she was reflected in.

"Get a grip." He heard her say out loud. She then pawed through her cosmetic case and pulled out her toothbrush. She brushed her teeth, packed up her case and left the room. As soon as the light turned off, so did the camera. Alex pushed eject and went back to the production tent.

"Why haven't you helped her?" Alex demanded of Eddie after bursting into his tent.

"She didn't ask for it," he responded and went on, "besides, she signed the contract. She knew what the risks were when she agreed to be on the show, she can't touch us".

Alex left the tent. He couldn't believe all Eddie was worried about was being sued. He'd surely seen the scrapes. Why didn't he care and why didn't he do anything about it? Alex figured there wasn't much that he could do about it. If he admitted to Sammi that he knew about her being hurt, she'd know that there not only was a camera in the bathroom, but he had access to watch. He didn't want anyone's behavior at the camp changing because they knew he was watching them. Besides, it was written in his contract that he couldn't say a word about it to anyone. He would just have to deal. If Sammi was strong enough to grit her teeth and push through her pain, the least he could do would be to honor that strength and not bring attention to her pain. It might kill him, but he'd do it.

Susan Stoker

Chapter Eight

The next morning the women's camp was a hub of activity. The eight women who had won the competition the day before were going to meet Al and were very excited. They were running around, trying to make sure they wore the correct outfit, their hair was just right and that the outfits they'd chosen were appropriate. Sammi once again retreated to the overlook up the hill. Her side didn't hurt as much this morning, but she knew it would be tough to do any sort of strenuous exercise without it being painful. She knew she wouldn't get any sympathy from anyone, and besides, it wasn't as if she was going to get any kind of tropical disease from the scratches. Sammi turned back toward the camp just in time to see the bus pull up and the eight giddy women climb aboard. She shrugged and turned back toward the amazing view of the Outback. She was sure she and the other women would hear all about the visit with Al when the ladies got back to camp later.

* * *

Alex watched as the bus pulled up and the women almost tumbled out in their haste to get to him. He braced himself as all eight women surrounded him. They were all almost talking at once. Finally, he laughed and said, "One at a time, ladies."

One woman leaned up and kissed him on the cheek, closer to his lips than he was comfortable with, and said, "Hi, I'm Missy."

One by one the other women followed suit. Alex felt like he was going to suffocate with all the different perfumes the women were wearing. The smell of the perfume was overwhelming and completely out of place in the beauty that was the Outback. He heard their names as if he was in a box…"Lori, Jennie, Kiki, Candi…" He remembered the conversation the day before with Sammi about everyone's name ending in "ie" and he almost laughed out loud. He wasn't surprised that his thoughts turned to Sammi. He'd been thinking about her all night and wondering how she was doing. He forced himself back to the present and to concentrate on the eight women around him.

After the initial introductions were over Alex fell into the same routine as the day before. He met with each woman one at a time and then halfway through the meetings they had brunch. Then it was back to the conversations.

After lunch Alex first met with Courtnee.

"Hello. Courtnee, isn't it?" Alex said with a smile.

Courtnee was obviously happy that he'd remembered her name.

"Yes, that's right. Hi, Al. I can't tell you how happy I am to be here and to finally get time alone with you."

Alex wondered if she knew how corny that sounded. "Where are you from again? I think you said in your video that you were from Florida?"

"Yes," Courtnee gushed. "Pensacola. I just love it there, I have the cutest little house, it's right on the beach, and…"

Alex tuned her out. Their conversation was much

like the other women's. They talked on and on about themselves and didn't really once ask about him or about what he liked to do. Finally, he decided to see if she would talk about the incident yesterday.

"Uh, so, Courtnee…you must have gotten a lot of fish yesterday in order to be in the top eight, huh?" Alex asked, pretending interest.

"Yes, although I would have gotten more if Jennie hadn't pushed me out of the way of the barrel at the last second!" Courtnee exclaimed. "It really wasn't fair. I'd reached the barrel first!"

"What about Sammi?" Alex asked.

"What about her?" Courtnee responded. "She didn't have nearly as many fish as we did, so it didn't matter if she got that last fish or not. It wasn't my fault that she fell in the river. If she wasn't so clumsy she wouldn't have." It was obvious Courtnee knew exactly what he was asking about. If Alex wasn't mistaken, he could detect a hint of defensiveness in her tone.

Alex couldn't believe what he'd just heard. She honestly thought it wasn't her fault, or at least felt no remorse over knocking Sammi into the water.

"Mmmm." Alex couldn't think of anything else to respond to Courtnee that wouldn't come out as totally inappropriate.

That didn't seem to matter to her. She just kept on talking. Finally it was time for Alex to have a one-on-one with another contestant. She leaned up to Alex's ear and whispered, "I had a great time, and I think you're really hot. I know we can be red hot together…see ya later, sweetheart." With that Courtnee reached up and kissed Alex right on the lips.

As she walked away Alex ran the back of his hand

across his lips. It was going to be a long afternoon.

* * *

There was a lot of speculation back at the camp. The women from the day before wanted to know what went on in the meet-and-greet and it seemed like everyone was trying to one-up everyone else in their stories about what went on in their individual meetings. Camp was actually quite boring. There wasn't a lot to do, and it was hot during the day. It was really too hot to sit in the tents, but it was too hot to sit out in the sun as well. Finally, about three o'clock, Robert and Eddie sauntered into camp.

"Gather 'round, ladies," he said pompously. "It's time to see who the next lady going home will be." And with that Al was brought out from behind some trees. They were told they were all going to be walking a bit to get to where the competition would be. So they all trudged along after Robert and Eddie. Nikki and Kathi did their best to monopolize Al's attention. They were on either side of him and grabbed onto his arms. Sam followed along near the back of the pack. She wasn't sure that she was up to much physical movement because her side felt like it was on fire. It started to hurt more as the day went on. She figured she'd play it by ear and see what happened when they got to wherever it was they were going.

They came upon a large clearing that had been set up to look like a rodeo circle. There was a little platform on one side with chairs set up. The circle was about one hundred feet in diameter, surrounded by large boulders. The women were instructed to stand in two lines in the middle of the circle while Al was seated on the podium. *This can't be good.* Sam thought.

"Welcome to the first challenge where the loser will be saying goodbye to Al and goodbye to Australia," Robert bellowed as if they were all standing on the other side of the circle rather than right in front of him.

"Today's challenge involves your wits as well as speed and strength." With that the producers freed two large pigs into the circle. Immediately Courtnee and Missy started screeching at the top of their lungs. The pigs ran around the outside of the circle, snorting and grunting. When Sam looked closer it looked as if they were drooling too. She suppressed a smile. Finally Robert got everyone's attention again.

"There are now fifteen of you left. There will be fourteen pigs released into the circle. The object is to grab a pig and get it to the chute at the NE side of the circle. Once you've gotten a pig to the chute you can't go back into the circle. The lady left without a pig will be the one who has to go home. You have ten minutes to figure out a strategy."

With that most of the women immediately started complaining. They didn't know they would be pig wrestling today. Many wore totally inappropriate clothes and shoes. Katie was even wearing a pair of heels! Sam laughed to herself. *This ought to be good.* She wasn't altogether sure that she'd be able to hold on to one of the pigs with her side hurting like it did, but she sure wasn't going to let some of those other women make her look like a loser on National Television!

Alex looked on from the platform. His thoughts were running along the same lines as Sam's were. He figured it would make for great TV to see the women running around in their high heels and fancy clothes, trying to corral a pig. While the pigs didn't weigh much more than twenty pounds each, it would be interesting to see their strategies for corralling them. Alex looked at Sam. He once again noticed that she certainly wasn't as model pretty as the other women, but she also wasn't as "made up" as they were. She was wearing sensible shoes with jeans and a T-shirt. He watched as she stood in one place and surveyed the circle, the chute and even the two pigs that were still in the circle. She seemed stiff, but Alex knew it was because of the scrapes on her side. Not once did he see her talk to Eddie or Robert. Al knew this challenge would probably hurt her side, but he knew with one hundred percent certainty that she would suck it up and not say anything to anyone about how she was feeling. It concerned him because he didn't want to see her lose. She was, so far, one of the main reasons this farce of a show was bearable.

Finally, Robert climbed up the short set of stairs to stand on the platform with him. There were also several camera operators on the platform as well as roaming around the circle, filming the women from all angles. The women were all placed at one side of the circle. At Robert's "GO" the rest of the pigs were released and the women were off and running…well, some were running. Some of the women immediately ran toward the pigs, screeching, and others just kinda stood still as if in shock and not knowing what they should do.

For a few minutes it didn't look like anyone would be able to get any of the pigs into the "end zone," but finally Jennie from Montana coaxed/pulled/pushed one into the zone. She let out a whoop for joy and was escorted to the outside of the circle. The race was on. Slowly, one by one, pigs were corralled. Ashley, Candi, Lori, and Brandi all corralled a pig. Alex's attention turned to Sam. She was slowly walking toward a pig. She'd gotten it close to the chute when Courtnee came up next to her and "tripped," shoving Sam to the ground. Courtnee then got behind the pig and pushed with all her might until the pig went running toward the chute, squealing the entire way. Courtnee had gotten her pig...at Sam's expense.

Alex surged to his feet. He'd seen the whole thing and knew that Courtnee had definitely cheated. Of course, Eddie and Robert said nothing. Alex clenched his teeth and silently cheered Sammi on. He willed her to look at him, to see that he was rooting for her. To try to give her the strength to corral another pig. He glared at Courtnee and didn't care if she saw it.

Sam was furious. Her side hurt, she was dirty, had a horrible headache and now that bitch Courtnee had stolen her pig and was laughing, *laughing*, at her. She almost called it quits right there. This wasn't worth it. Why did she want to fight over some guy who probably was laughing at her right this minute? Sam reluctantly looked toward the podium and at Al. He was no longer sitting, but standing and it looked like he was scowling at her. Sam did a double take, why was he mad at her? What did she do? Then she looked a bit closer and it seemed like Al wasn't looking at her after all, but watching Courtnee greet the other women on the other side of the circle. Then he turned his eyes on her. Seeing that she was looking at him, he gave her a small smile and nod of his head. Sam sighed. *Shit, I guess I have to get one of these stupid pigs after all.* She wasn't going to let Courtnee win and have the satisfaction of knowing she had gotten her kicked off. So, ignoring the pain in her side, Sam set out to capture another stupid pig. She had no doubt that she would succeed. She had quite a bit of motivation.

With Sam's success, finally it came down to one pig left in the circle, and two women. Kimmie and Kiki were fighting for all they were worth to try to make sure they weren't the loser. It seemed to be an even match. Finally, it seemed as if the pig was getting tired of the game. He wanted to join his buddies on the other side of the circle. He took a sharp turn and started running right for the corral. Kiki was closer to the chute and managed to grab onto the pig as it ran past her and right into the corral. Kimmie was left without a pig.

"That's not fair!" she screeched. "She didn't capture it, it ran right by her!" Kiki was grinning like a ninny while Kimmie continued to complain.

Robert told all the women to line back up in their original spots. Al came down off the podium and stood next to Robert. He spared a quick glance at Sammi and managed to give her an inconspicuous head nod.

"It looks like you are left without a pig, Kimmie," Robert began, "you're going to have to say goodbye to Al and the other women right here and now. Your belongings will be brought to you later. Do you have anything to say?" Darn right Kimmie had something to say…

70

"You're all a bunch of losers. You'd cheat and lie to your own mother if it would serve your purpose. If you were dying of thirst I wouldn't give you a drink of water!" And with that she flounced away from the group toward the waiting car.

Sam couldn't help it. She laughed, out loud. It was too much. It was too much like the first season of *Survivor* when the one contestant said practically the same thing to the woman finalist. What drama, what flair…but she also knew it would make great television.

Robert seemed to finally come out of the trance that he was in after Kimmie's departure.

"Okay, ladies, you've earned the right to stick around another day. It's time to go back to camp, and you'll meet with Al later today."

With that, Al, Eddie, and Robert left, and the women walked back to their camp. Of course, once they got there it was a free-for-all as the women all tried to fight for the shower. It seemed they didn't mind there wasn't any hot water anymore. They all wanted to get the pig smell off of them and get ready for their meet-and-greet with Al later on that day.

Sam was finally able to take her turn in the shower. It seemed like she'd been wet more in the last few days than she'd been in her "real" life back in Albuquerque. She didn't mind. She'd always been a good swimmer. She'd been on the water polo team in high school, so she felt comfortable in and around water. When Sam walked out of the little bathroom building, she didn't see much movement around the camp. The women were mostly in the tents just hanging out, waiting for Robert or someone to come and get them.

I can't believe them. Sam thought to herself. *They're in Australia and they're sitting around in tents, waiting to hang out with some guy, whatever.* And with that Sam decided she'd take a walk back up the rise. It wasn't a long walk, and she could still see the camp from where she was. It was simply beautiful. How she'd love to explore a bit, Sam felt like she was "tied" to the camp. It wasn't fair, here she was in one of the most beautiful parts of the world and she was waiting with thirteen other women to meet the guy they were supposed to be "dating." She couldn't deny that she was attracted to him and that he was hot, but it was depressing that she was in completion for him. Sam sighed and tried to put the whole show out of her mind, then looked behind her and saw the ever-present Kina with the camera and smirked. She'd make Kina earn her keep today. There certainly wasn't much to film back at camp. That had to be why Kina was following her. Sam noticed she wasn't filmed nearly as much as the other women were, but it didn't bother her in the least. *Let them have all the camera time.* Sam started off down the hill. She didn't know how long it would be before they were supposed to go and visit with Al, but she needed this. She needed to get away from the other women for a while. Most of them weren't bad, but they did grate on her nerves. They were just so different. For about the hundredth time Sam wondered how *she* had gotten on the show. She convinced herself that it was either a mistake or they needed some comic relief.

The sun was hot, but it really was pretty. Sam walked on, almost oblivious to Kina trudging along behind her. Every once in a while she heard Kina mumble to herself, but Kina didn't stop her or talk to her. After all, that was against the rules. Eventually, after about twenty minutes of walking, Sam stopped under a large tree, sat down, leaned against the trunk and shut her eyes, just breathing in the clean air and enjoying the fact that she was in Australia. After a few minutes Sam heard Kina sit down next to her. Sam peeked out of one eye and saw Kina had put down the camera and was looking at her.

"What?" Sam asked.

"I don't get you," Kina responded. Sam couldn't help it, she laughed.

"I know. I'm a loner, what can I say? Look around, look at how beautiful all this is. I would choose this over sitting around talking about how much I miss the mall any day".

With that, Sam put her head back against the tree trunk and shut her eyes again, not waiting to see how Kina reacted to her bluntness.

Finally, she heard Kina say, "I like you, Sammi."

Sam smiled, but didn't say anything. *At least one person seems to like me.*

Sam and Kina sat under the tree for about thirty minutes. Sam was half asleep when she heard Kina's voice.

"You're missing it, you know," Kina finally spoke up again.

"Huh? What am I missing?" Sam asked.

"The meet-and-greet," Kina responded. "They left ten minutes ago."

With that Sam leaped up.

"Oh, shit, I can't believe they left without me!"

She looked at Kina again and saw she was back to her camerawoman mode. The camera was up and pointed at her again. Sam figured it wouldn't make any sense to go running back to camp, especially if the women had truly already left. They obviously knew where she was, Kina had some sort of communication with them since she knew they'd already left. *Screw it.* Sam thought. *If I've already missed the bus I might as well explore some more.* And she set off walking again. *I won't go far, just a bit more.*

Chapter Nine

The bus pulled up to the clearing where the producers had set up a sort of "living room." There were tree stumps around for seating and a few tables set up around the clearing. Alex watched as the women climbed off the bus. He was immediately surrounded by all of the women who seemed to all be talking at once again.

I can't wait until more of them are gone. Alex thought and immediately felt guilty. It'll be much easier to talk to them and get to know everyone when there are fewer of them! Soon enough they were sitting around and having a pretty good conversation. He was, of course, the center of attention and he allowed the talk to flow around him. The women were definitely on their best behavior today and they all looked gorgeous. He wasn't sure how they accomplished it out here in the wilds of the backcountry, but somehow they all looked like they were sitting down at a party in New York or something.

After about forty minutes of talking, Alexander could identify most of the women, he could even tell most of them apart. He knew who Courtnee was, of course, and Missy was also pretty forward, so he knew her. He actually was beginning to like Amy and Jennie. They seemed a little less harsh and spoiled than the others. They weren't quite as "citified" as Katie or Kiki. Of course, he knew Sammi as well…as soon as the thought crossed his mind he realized he hadn't seen her. Before he could stop himself he found himself asking the group, "Where's Sammi?" The other women looked around and shrugged, then continued their conversations. They didn't seem to care. All they cared about was that they were here with him and trying to get his attention.

Alex started to worry. Why wasn't she there? Had they kicked her off and hadn't told him? He couldn't believe it had taken him so long to realize she wasn't there. She really did stick out, not in a bad way, but she stuck out nonetheless. The next hour was the longest hour he'd spent in the Outback. He couldn't stop worrying about it. Finally, the visiting time was over and the women got back on the bus to return to their camp. Upon arriving at the production site, Alex found Eddie.

"Where's Sammi?" he asked impatiently. He'd spent the last hour and a half worrying about where she might be. Was she hurt? Was she gone? If she was gone how would he be able to find her again?

Eddie looked at him and said, "She missed the bus at camp, so we left. Thought it would be a good lesson for the other women and for her. She just can't wander off. She's here for the show, and besides, someone could get hurt." Alex couldn't believe it. Eddie was trying to teach her a lesson?

"What do you mean wander off?" Alexander asked in a low voice.

"Just what I said," Eddie said in an annoyed tone. "Look, she decided she wanted to go for a little walk. Kina is following her. Nothing is happening."

"What did she do when she realized she'd been left behind?" Alex asked.

"Don't know. They're still out there. I'm in touch

with Kina. I let her know that the bus had left. I don't know if Sammi knows she missed the bus. She'll come back in her own time. She can't get lost, Kina is filming her and we can watch the tapes. Calm down, Al, there are fourteen women left. You've lots of time to make your choice." And with that Eddie was called away.

Alex wondered where the hell Sammi was and what the hell she was thinking wandering around by herself. If he was honest with himself he was upset that he'd missed another chance to see her and get to know her.

* * *

In actuality Sam wasn't doing much wandering. She was content to stroll around and take long breaks under the enormous trees. She was enjoying watching the different species of birds and small animals running around. The only thing she was upset about was that she didn't have a camera with her. She would've loved to be able to take pictures of what she was experiencing so she could share them with her family and friends. After a while she decided she'd better go back to the camp. She didn't know if she'd be in trouble for missing the bus and the meet-and-greet, but she figured she'd better be back at camp by the time the others got off the bus or she might really be in trouble.

After one of her breaks under a beautiful shade tree, Sam stood up and waited for Kina to get in position before she started back toward the camp. She'd learned that the best thing to do with the cameras was to let them film the way they wanted to so they'd leave her alone. Sam waited until Kina got in front of her and started walking backward so she could get a good frontal view of her walking. They both heard it at the same time…it was the unmistakable sound of a rattlesnake. Sam didn't know what species of snakes the Outback had, but that sound couldn't be a good thing. It was universal for danger. Kina stopped in her tracks, camera still on her shoulder, pointed toward Sam.

"Don't move, Kina," Sam said. "It's right by your foot."

Kina froze even more if that was possible. A sad little whimper escaped from her throat. "Oh God," she moaned.

"Kina, I'm going to try to get it away from you…don't move whatever you do. Maybe it'll think you're a tree or something." Sam had no idea what she was talking about. Some scientist would probably scoff at what she'd said, but she hoped Kina would believe her and feel calmer about the entire situation. Sam found a large stick. She'd watched reruns of that famous Australian guy on TV more times than she could count. She knew there was a way to pin the head to the ground and pick it up, but she sure as hell wasn't going to try that. Sam only knew she had to get that snake away from Kina's legs. She didn't know what she'd do if the thing decided that it wanted a snack!

The snake was huge. About eight feet long and its head looked about as big as one of her basset hound's heads back at home. Sam started to sweat. *This is all my fault.* She thought. *If I hadn't walked away from camp Kina wouldn't be in this situation.*

78

Sam walked around Kina and the snake turned to follow her movements. Good. Sam thought. 'It's watching me and not paying attention to Kina, whose legs it was almost wrapped around.

"Kina, it's almost wrapped around your legs, but its attention is on me. Don't put the camera down, don't move. I'm going to start backing up and hopefully it'll follow me. I have no idea if this will work or not, but I hope like hell it will. When you feel it slide away take *slow* steps in the direction you're facing. That'll put distance between you and it."

"What are you going to do?" Kina whispered. "If it follows you, how are you going to get away from it?"

"I don't know, but at least it won't be near you," Sam responded, still feeling guilty for putting Kina in this position in the first place. Then Sam said flippantly, "And besides, it'll make for great television so be sure that you're filming…contestant wanders out of camp by herself and gets attacked by a killer snake…think of the ratings!" She chuckled uneasily.

While Sam had been talking to Kina she'd been slowly backing up. It seemed to be working. The snake was following her. Inch by inch it unfurled itself from around Kina. It definitely didn't look happy, and it hadn't stopped rattling its tail the entire time. Kina took one step forward, then another…finally, she was able to turn around and face Sam and the snake. She took aim with her camera.

Sam and the snake were facing each other. Sam was armed with only a stick and the snake looked agitated. Sam started talking to the snake, not really knowing what she was saying. "Okay, Mr. Snake, we're sorry that we disturbed you. We'll be on our way, okay? You don't need to bite me. I probably don't taste very good. Now, some of the women at camp are more your style, you'd love them. How about just turning around and going home…just like I want to do. I'll just be on my way, no harm no foul. I promise not to come down this way and bother you again if you just let me go now…okay? Niiiiice snake…" Sam was backing up slowly, never taking her eyes off of the snake. Thankfully, it decided that escape was probably the better option and it slithered away into the underbrush nearby.

Sam looked up at Kina, and thus into the camera.

"That was a close one…are you okay, Kina?" Kina didn't respond.

"Oh, okay, we are back to the rules," Sam said with disappointment.

With that Sam turned her back on the camera and started the way they'd come. *It would've been nice for her to at least say thank you.* Suddenly, she didn't feel very good. She knew it was a reaction to the stress and fear and probably the heat as well. She darted toward a bush and threw up what little she'd eaten that day.

"Ugh, gross," she said out loud. "That is the worst."

Sam wiped a shaky hand across her mouth and trudged on toward the camp, not daring to look at Kina or the camera. She was sure there was now an up-close-and-personal shot of her losing her stomach contents that would surely be shown on National Television in the not-so-distant future. Lovely.

Sam continued to shake as she walked. She thought about what had happened and what had almost happened to Kina. It was times like this that she really missed being a part of a couple. While she felt she was an independent modern woman, there was something to be said about being held safe and comfortable in a man's arms. She took a deep breath and continued on toward the camp to find out how much trouble she was in.

What had started out as a beautiful day and a beautiful walk had turned sour. She'd missed the bus and was probably in trouble for that. She'd talked to one of the camera operators, which was against the rules, so she was probably in trouble for that. Then the snake incident, which was scarier in person than she imagined it could be, *and* she humiliated herself in front of the camera and probably in front of millions of people. She *knew* that incident would show up on screen and she'd never live it down with her friends or her coworkers back in Albuquerque. She trudged on, lost in her thoughts while Kina followed behind.

Sam and Kina finally made it back to camp. She hadn't been able to arrive before the women had gotten back after all. She'd obviously been wandering around in the Outback for longer than she expected. The women were hanging around, talking about Al and his reactions to each of them and their conversations.

Missy turned to Sam and said snidely, "Where were you, Miss Tarzan? You're in big trouble, you know? You missed it. But don't worry. Al didn't miss you and neither did we. Right, ladies?" And with that most of the other women laughed and giggled.

Sam was too tired to care and was still dealing with the after effects of adrenaline that her body was producing as a result of the fear of the snake and what might have happened to Kina. She looked around and saw Kina getting into a golf cart, probably to go back to the production camp to talk about how she'd broken the rules. Sam ignored Missy and the other women, went back to the tent and lay down on her cot. What would happen now? She was worried, and was glad that she could finally lie down. She replayed the incident in her head. It'd been a close call. Kina had almost stepped directly on the snake. If she'd done that she would have been bitten for sure, and then what would Sam have done? There was no way that she could have carried her all the way back to the camp. She'd put someone's life on the line for her own selfish desires. It wouldn't happen again.

Chapter Ten

Alex watched Kina get out of the golf cart and go straight to Eddie's office. He remembered the producer said that Kina was with Sammi. He followed Kina into the tent in time to hear Eddie bellow, "Where the hell were you guys?!? She missed the bus! How come you didn't tell us where you were when we asked?!?" He sounded more upset now about the situation than when Alex talked to him earlier. Then he didn't seem like it mattered or that he cared about Sammi missing the bus.

All the camera operators wore little two way microphones. That way they could communicate with production at all times.

Kina responded, "I couldn't. We were out in the middle of nowhere. If I'd started talking to you the camera would've picked it up and the footage would've been ruined."

Eddie sighed. He knew Kina was right, and there was nothing more that he hated than great footage ruined by the chit chat of a camera operator.

Kina continued, "She went for a walk, I followed her. She took a nap by a tree, then we started back toward camp. On our way back she saved my life." Eddie snapped to attention.

"What?!?" he yelled. "Did you get it on tape?"

"Sort of," Kina said.

Kina didn't say anything else, but held out the tape that had been in her camera that day. Eddie snatched it out of her hand faster than the snake could have bitten her today and put it into the player.

With Alex, Eddie, and Kina watching, the tape was played. They watched Sammi's face as she realized what the problem was. They heard her talking to Kina. The camera was glued to Sammi as Kina stood still above the snake. Then they saw Sammi walk out of the line of vision and continue to tell Kina what she was going to do and what Kina should do. The camera microphone had picked up Kina's frantic breathing. Finally, the camera moved and swung back around to Sammi and the snake. Alex about had a heart attack. Sammi was leaning over, waving a stick, trying to get that huge snake to follow her. Eventually, the snake slithered off.

"Damn, that's good footage," Eddie said, "but since the cameras aren't supposed to exist, we can't use it." Alex just looked at him incredulously.

"Sammi was talking to the camera operator, and Kina was talking back, that's not a part of the "reality" of this show. We can't use it." Eddie defended himself as Alex glared at him.

Eddie continued, "Good job today, Kina, get some rest and you'll be back on her tomorrow. Maybe she'll feel more comfortable around you and tell you juicy secrets on tape that we can use." He grabbed the tape out of the machine and held it out to Kina. "Take this back to the production tent." And with that, he shooed Alex and Kina out of the tent.

As they walked away, Kina turned to Alex and said, "She really did save my life, Al, I was about to bolt or do something stupid and she calmed me down and led that snake away. I could feel it slithering around my legs and knew that it was going to bite me any second." She shuddered, then continued, "That wasn't all that happened out there, you should watch the entire tape." She handed the tape they'd just watched to Alex.

"Is she really all right?" Alex asked urgently.

"She was really quiet afterward and had a bad moment or two, but she's okay." Kina reassured him.

Alex took the tape back to his tent and watched Sammi's entire afternoon. She looked really peaceful resting against the tree and he could see that she really loved being out in nature. She seemed really relaxed until Kina almost stepped on the snake. He observed again her facial expressions and watched as she tried to lead the snake away from Kina. It was just as scary the second time he saw it as it was the first time. While he was scared to death for her, he was also proud. She'd handled the situation with a sense of calm. She didn't panic, she did what she needed to do. There was nothing he wanted more than to hold her and comfort her, and that freaked him out a little bit. He wasn't like this. He never felt like this about a woman this quickly before. Hell, he really didn't know her that well, but there was something about her.

Alex watched as Sammi continued walking back toward the camp. She wasn't looking around her at the scenery like she did on the way out. He thought he could even see her shaking. Then he saw her dart to a bush and throw up. After that she wiped her mouth and continued on her way without even looking at the camera.

Alex was stunned. He couldn't believe what he'd just seen. He didn't know many people that would be able to handle that kind of stress and not collapse. He was surprised that it had taken her so long to lose it. He wished he could talk to her about what happened, but again, he knew no one was to know that he had access to the show's tapes. He sighed and again felt the urge to wrap Sammi up in his arms and not let go. What a predicament. He honestly admired her. Yes, she'd wandered off on her own, which wasn't that smart of a thing to do, but in a crisis she had held herself together and not fallen apart. He couldn't image any of the other women doing the same. And after she'd thrown up she didn't throw a hissy fit, she just continued on her way. Sammi certainly was an interesting woman. One that Alex knew he'd like to get to know a lot better.

Chapter Eleven

The next day started out like any of the others at the camp. There was a mad dash for the bathroom and for the shower followed by a flurry of hairspray, makeup and bickering. The women apparently decided that cold showers weren't that bad when the alternative was no shower. Fourteen women all intent on getting the same man was wearing thin, however. Like usual, Sam waited until most everyone was done with the bathroom before taking her turn. She'd slept in later than usual this morning, but she was so exhausted from the stress from the day before that she couldn't make herself get up. *I wonder what fun and games the producers have in store for us today.* She put her hair up in a clip and left the bathroom.

Soon the bus pulled up to the camp. Eddie and Robert got out of a golf cart and assembled all the women in their customary lines.

"I have good news and bad news," Robert intoned. "The good news is that no one is going home today." He paused to allow the cameras time to pan over the women who were cheering and smiling. "The bad news is that today and tomorrow you'll work harder than most of you have before in your lives." The cheering stopped as if a TV was unplugged suddenly.

"What do you mean?" Candi asked. "What kind of job could there be out here in the middle of nowhere?"

"Well," Robert continued with a smirk, as if he knew what he was about to say would ruin the women's day. "Part of Al's life is to work on his ranch,

Susan Stoker

so today and tomorrow you will be working on a cattle ranch. Your jobs will involve all the daily activities that are usually undertaken on the ranch. You need to pack an overnight bag with outdoor clothes and sneakers, or comfortable shoes if you brought them, and we'll leave in about half an hour."

As soon as Robert stepped off the podium and was back in his golf cart heading out, the girls started complaining.

"I can't believe this," Missy snapped. "I've never been around a *cow* in all my life, how can I work on a ranch when I don't know what I'm doing?"

"It doesn't make sense," Brandi chimed in. "What are we, slave labor? This was supposed to be fun!"

Kathi exclaimed, "I better not break a nail!"

As the women continued on with their complaining, Sam wandered back to her tent to pack her belongings. Since she shared it with some of the other contestants she couldn't get away from their mumblings, but she did her best to block them out. Courtnee nudged her in the side as she was packing.

"Are you going to run away again, Miss Bitch?" she asked nastily. "It doesn't matter to me one way or another since there's no way in Hell you're going to last much longer. Why don't you just quit now?"

"Why do you say that?" Sam asked, knowing full well she wouldn't like the answer, but trying to stand up for herself nonetheless.

"Look at you," Courtnee continued, "You're short and dumpy. You have no fashion sense and you don't wear makeup." Looking around, she noticed the other women watching and it fueled the venom spewing out of her mouth. "You don't belong here. You aren't in

88

Al's league. He needs someone who will look good by his side. Someone with his wealth needs a beautiful woman on his arm, and you certainly aren't it. I mean really, why are you even on this show? You don't fit in."

Sam stood there, looking at Courtnee and the other women who were watching from a small distance away.

"How would you know what he needs?" Sam asked. "None of us know Al, we've met him what twice? For that matter you don't know me. So what that I don't look like you guys? I know I'm not beautiful, but that doesn't diminish my value as a person. Maybe I'm just here for the free trip to Australia." Then she glared at Courtnee. "We don't like each other, that's not big news, but Courtnee, I'll stand up for myself, so let's agree to stay away from each other and let the game unfold. I'll stay out of your way and you stay out of mine."

With that Sam turned away and continued to pack. She knew she'd made an enemy, but she just wasn't up to taking her crap like she usually would do in a similar situation back in "her" world. Just because she wasn't five feet eleven inches tall and she weighed more than a seven-year-old child would, didn't mean that she wasn't a good person.

Their thirty minutes was up and they all piled back on the bus. The ride to the ranch was about forty-five minutes long. Sam had no idea where they were going, all she knew was that it was dusty and they seemed to be in the middle of nowhere. Finally, they saw a line of trees in the distance and buildings slowly began to take shape. They pulled into a large driveway circle in front of the most beautiful house Sam had ever seen. It was huge! Three stories high with a beautiful front porch. There were rocking chairs set out on the porch. There were dogs running around the yard and property. It was wonderful, beautiful, and Sam couldn't wait to get out and meet whoever was lucky enough to live in such a wonderful place.

The women filed out of the bus and were instructed to stand in their customary two lines. Robert stood in his usual spot and began talking.

"Welcome to the Choxie Ranch. There are over eight hundred acres on the property and you'll begin working right away. There are many different types of chores, and we'll draw from a hat to see which you'll be doing. We'll switch off later today and in the morning. Are there any questions before we begin?"

Ashley raised her hand and asked, "Will Al be joining us?"

The question was one that all the women really wanted to know the answer to. They wanted to know if he'd be there to watch their supreme efforts on their chores. They wanted to know what kind of effort they'd have to put forth. If he was there, they'd try harder, if not then they'd get by with the minimum that they could.

"Al will be joining you later tonight. He'll spend time doing each of the chores with you. Now, the chores that you'll be assisting with are helping in the kitchen, working with the maids, mucking out the stalls, riding the fence line, feeding the animals, and weeding the garden."

There was complete silence from the women. Sam wanted to laugh. It was too perfect. She didn't really want to do any of those jobs, but she knew she was in far better shape to do them than the other spoiled contestants. She cleaned her own house, fed her three dogs twice a day every day, cooked her own meals…she knew that most of the others probably had hired help to do all those things. She looked around and saw the shock on the other women's faces. She again had to stifle a giggle.

They started to draw jobs from the hat one by one. Ashley and Kathi pulled kitchen duty first. Missy, Brandi, and Katie got maid duty. Cindee, Sammi, and Amy were going to be mucking out the stalls. Nikki and Lori were going to be riding the fence lines. Kiki and Courtnee would be feeding the animals, while Jennie and Candi would be weeding the huge garden out back.

Sam figured she'd get the "poop" job…with three dogs at home it seemed as if she was constantly picking up poo at home, so why shouldn't she do it when she was on vacation too? It was actually pretty funny. She figured she could've gotten stuck with worse people than Amy and Cindee to work with as well.

The women all went off to do their respective chores. They hadn't seen Al yet, and they weren't sure when he would show up and who he would "help" first. Sammi, Cindee, and Amy were brought into a huge barn. There were stalls alongside stalls alongside stalls. No wonder there were three of them assigned to this chore. Cindee and Amy immediately scrunched up their noses at the pungent smell emanating from the stalls. *It is a bit strong.* Sam thought. But *what did I expect, it's a barn!*

91

They were handed long pitchforks and given a quick lesson on how to shovel the horse droppings out of the stalls and into a large bin. Most of the horses were out in the pasture so they would have the place mostly to themselves. They were given gloves—which of course were too big for them—and set to work. Sam and Amy started on one side of the barn and Cindee started on the other.

The time went by pretty fast for Sam. The job was backbreaking, but not hard. All three of the women were sweating pretty hard. The barn was insulated, but the heat of the day combined with the hard shoveling was no match for the ceiling fans lazily circling above their heads. After about three hours the girls were told they were done for the day.

"Good job, ladies, I'm impressed," a cowboy named Henry told them. "I didn't expect you'd get as much done as you did. Thank you."

It *was* a job well done if Sam did say so herself. Together they'd mucked out all the stalls and had gotten a good start on spreading new hay as well. It wasn't perfect, they'd taken quite a few breaks to rest, but they'd done it. Henry told them they were to meet back out at the front of the house where they'd assembled when they'd first arrived. They trudged back out front and saw that the other women were slowly gathering. The women who were working in the house didn't look too much the worse for wear, but the women who worked outside in the sun looked very bedraggled.

Once everyone had assembled, Robert spoke, "Hopefully you enjoyed your first few hours here at the Choxie Ranch. I think we'd all like to hear about how your day went. I'd like for each group to come up and talk about how the job they did today and anything else interesting that happened. And since none of you got to work with Al today, he'd like to hear how things went as well."

Alex strode out of the house and stood next to Robert.

"This should be interesting," Sam muttered under her breath.

First up was the garden crew. Jennie and Candi went up to join Robert and Al. Both were a bit sunburned, but not too bad considering they were pretty tan to begin with.

Jennie started discussing how their day went. "Well, the garden is huge. There are flowers as well as vegetables. We were told what we should be looking for to pull, but it was a bit difficult since neither of us has really worked in a garden before. I guess we kept pulling the wrong thing. Candi actually pulled up something that she thought was a weed, but it turned out to be a vegetable!" At that Jennie giggled.

Candi interrupted, "Yeah, well, what about when you sat on a bunch of flowers to get a better grip on the weed that you were trying to pull?!?"

It seemed as if the light humor of the moment was gone. The competition was on. Candi and Jennie were not looking happy and were starting to glare at each other.

Alex broke the tension and said, "Did you enjoy your afternoon? Did you learn anything today?"

Jennie spoke up before Candi could. "Well, I wouldn't say it was *fun*, and I guess I learned that it's hard work and if you're going to have a big garden it'd

93

be best to make sure you hire someone to pull weeds!" She giggled again, and Sam couldn't help but roll her eyes. She looked at Al to see what he thought about what Jennie said, but his face was blank and she couldn't tell what he was thinking.

Next up was Nikki and Lori who talked about their "fence riding" experience. It didn't sound like they got very far. Neither had even been around horses before and so they were nervous and spent a lot of time walking the horses instead of riding them because of their inexperience and fright around the horses. They watched a few ranch hands check the fences and claimed they couldn't help because the gloves didn't fit them and it might mess up their manicures.

Next it was Sam, Cindee, and Amy's turn. Cindee spoke for them all and talked about how the barn was very smelly and hot and definitely not something she wanted to do. She even complained a bit about how they didn't even get to meet the horses, only dealt with their droppings! Sam couldn't stand it anymore. It seemed like the entire session was becoming one big complaint after another.

"It wasn't too bad," Sam piped up, interrupting Cindee's complaints. "Yes, it was hot, and yes it was definitely smelly, but it felt good to be able to help the animals by making sure they'd have a clean bed when they came home for the night." Sam looked at the faces of the women in front of her. Some looked bored, others looked indifferent, but a few looked at her with daggers in their eyes. Sam didn't know why, didn't know what she said that was so bad, but then she figured that the ones who were glaring at her didn't like her anyway, so no matter what she said they would probably do the same thing.

Missy, Brandi, and Katie were up next discussing their chores that they had to do around the house. Missy was appalled that she had to clean toilets. She said it was degrading and "icky." It didn't sound like the chores they had to do were too bad. And their description of the house was amazing. Sam wished she was able to walk around and examine the house. It was fascinating from the outside. She just knew it'd be just as beautiful inside.

Ashley and Kathi discussed the kitchen duties. They helped with the afternoon meal for the ranch hands. Apparently Kathi dropped and broke a platter, but the head cook assured her that it was okay. They claimed to have washed "thousands" of dishes— Ashley's words—and talked about how they had to mop the floor twice.

Last to go was Kiki and Courtnee whose job it was to feed the various animals around the farm. They gushed on and on for about twenty minutes about how cute all the animals were. They made it sound like they were angels who were feeding the starving animals. Sam noticed they didn't talk much about feeding the pigs. Sam had seen pigs being fed before, it wasn't a pretty thing.

Finally, they'd all told their stories and everyone got to know a bit about what each of the jobs entailed. They were tired and smelly and definitely ready to go inside and have a good meal and hopefully visit more with Al. Robert and Eddie, as usual, had another plan for them.

"Now that you've all finished your chores today you can go and find a place to sleep in the bunkhouse."

He pointed behind them toward the barn where off to the side there was a long rectangle shaped building. "There you will find your cots for the night as well as the kitchen where you'll need to fix your own food for the night. I wouldn't stay up too late, tomorrow will come soon enough."

Many of the women were flabbergasted. They weren't going to be allowed to sleep in the house tonight? What was this? How would Al get to know them and how would they get to know him better if they were stuck in the bunkhouse with each other? As it usually happens when women get together in tight spaces for too long of a time, they were starting to grate on each other's nerves. Cliques were definitely forming. It was as if the battle lines had been drawn. They were like wild dogs circling their prey—which was Al. If they didn't get first "crack" at him, then they'd fight for what they believed was "theirs."

Sam was tired of the "game" already. It wasn't the work she was doing, it was the fact that she was expected to be just as eager to discuss Al at all times and that she was expected to fight for him and to do anything to "get" him. It just wasn't her style at all. She figured if a guy was going to like her, he was going to like her as she was. She shouldn't have to *fight* for a guy. She believed if a guy was having a hard time choosing between her and another woman, then he could have the other woman. She wanted a man who would walk into a room and the first thing he'd do would be to seek her out. Who'd walk into a room and have eyes only for her. She wanted a man who she wouldn't have to worry about where he was, if he came home from work late and who he was with.

Trust. She wanted complete trust in a partner. She knew she wasn't as gorgeous as the women she was surrounded by. She also knew that most likely she wouldn't make it past the next few eliminations. She had high self-esteem, but it was being battered a bit constantly being around the models as she was.

Sam followed the other women to the bunkhouse where their suitcases had been dropped off earlier in the day. There were seven bunk beds set up around the small room, with a small bathroom and a kitchen. Missy immediately tried to take charge.

"Who's going to cook? It looks like we have food here," she said, looking at the other women expectantly. "Although it looks like we only have the fixings for pasta...anyone want that?" Of course, most of the women were horrified at the thought of eating all those carbs and ruining their diets. Sam was hungry. She'd spent most of the day working hard, she loved pasta, and she figured that if she was going to eat she'd better volunteer to cook. So Sam started getting out pots and ingredients to make the meal.

Susan Stoker

Chapter Twelve

"So what did you think of them?" Alex asked his aunt Nancy. Nancy and her husband owned the Choxie Ranch. Nancy had married an Australian and raised her children, Alex's cousins, there on the ranch. They were now all gone, the kids moved away and her husband passed away a few years ago. Eddie figured that this was a great opportunity to shake up the "game" a bit. It was going to be Nancy's job to tell the producers who the next woman would be to leave. She was to get to know as many of the women as she could. She'd watch the tapes of the women doing their chores with Alex. She would also meet the women who were working in the house in person. She wouldn't get to meet them all in person, but she would get to meet most of them.

"Where in the world did they find these women?" Nancy asked Alex. "They have no clue. They all look like Barbie dolls."

Alex agreed, "I thought the same thing. I haven't gotten to know them all very well yet, but they seem to be nice."

"Nice?" Nancy asked incredulously. "That isn't a word that I'd have imagined you would use when discussing beautiful women!" They both laughed and settled down to watch the tapes of the day.

Two hours later the duo had enough. It was obvious that the women were out of their element. Most tried to make the best out of a bad situation, but it was clear that some of them just weren't trying. The three most obvious were Katie, Nikki, and Candi. They did everything that they could do to get out of work and to let others do most of it.

"Come on Alex," Nancy said. "Let's get some chow and hit the sack. Five am is going to come up pretty fast for our city-slickers!"

At exactly five in the morning the women were awakened by a loud clanging. It was one of the ranch hands standing outside the bunk house, banging against a metal trash can.

"Time to get up, ladies, you have twenty minutes before you need to be up in the clearing for breakfast and then for your assignments for the day."

Sam had never heard such complaining and moaning in all her life. She was pretty sore, but she couldn't believe how the others were carrying on. You'd think they'd spent yesterday on a slave ship or something. Sam would kill for a shower, but she knew that wasn't going to happen with all the other women also clamoring for the use of the shower. Some were showering together at the same time. There was no way that Sam was going to stand next to one of the other women without any clothes on. That would be too much even for her ego.

They all trudged back to the clearing. Robert was there looking as clean cut and refreshed as ever. It was actually pretty annoying. They all sat down on benches that were put out for them as the kitchen staff brought out their breakfast. There was food piled up. It looked like they'd gone all out. There were eggs, bacon, sausage, pancakes, muffins, doughnuts, and even breakfast burritos. Sam laughed to herself, there was no way that some of those women would touch some of that food, but Sam was in heaven. She took a bit of everything, not knowing when they'd have the chance to eat again. Besides, she knew it would give her a bit of energy for the day's activities.

When everyone finished eating they all gathered in their respective places again and Robert began a speech about hard work and how they would be switching around jobs for the day. Al would be making the rounds and visiting each work team as they were doing their chores to see how they were getting along. Robert started pulling names out of the hat again.

Jennie and Kiki were going to work in the kitchen. Nikki, Cindee and Candi would be working with the maids. Brandi and Ashley would be riding the fence line. Amy and Kathi would be feeding the animals. Lori and Katie would be weeding, and Courtnee, Missy, and Sam would be mucking out the stalls.

Sam couldn't believe she got the same job as yesterday! It wasn't fair! But it wasn't like any of the other jobs were really all that good either. As far as things went she supposed it could be worse, but she wasn't happy with the fact that she'd have to work with Courtnee and Missy for the day. She knew that neither of them liked her, so she figured it would be a very long morning. No one seemed to notice or care that she'd done the same job the day before. Sam decided that if no one else was going to say anything, neither would she. It wasn't that big of a deal. As much as she wanted to get into the house and see if it was as beautiful on the inside as it was on the outside, she wasn't going to make someone switch with her. Mucking the stalls wasn't exactly a job that someone would want to switch her for. She'd have loved to have spent time with the animals, but she also knew there was no way in Hell that Kathi or Amy would switch with her. She couldn't blame them either.

They all left to attend to their perspective jobs. As Sam, Courtnee, and Missy arrived at the barn they saw that Al was already there. It looked like he'd be starting his day with them. Courtnee and Missy were beyond excited. They were glad they'd get to see him before they got all sweaty and smelly.

"Mornin', ladies," Al said with a drawl.

"Hi", "Hello", "Hey," they said in unison.

Courtnee sidled up to Al and asked, "Are you going to show us how to do this?"

Alex laughed and said, "Nope, that's Henry's job…Henry?"

With that Henry came over from the stall he'd been working in. Noticing Sam he frowned at her a bit and at her small shake of the head, he looked away and started explaining the best way to handle the pitchfork and the technique for throwing poo out of the stalls. When he was done with his explanations each of them grabbed a pitchfork and started working.

"Are you going to start with me first?" Missy asked Al while fluttering her eyelashes.

"Sure," Alex replied. He really hated mucking stalls, but it was funny to think of these women doing it. He laughed at Missy's attempts to pitch the poo over the stall and into the bin. She was actually pretty fun to work in the stalls with. She was funny and entertaining and certainly easy on the eyes. Soon he moved on to Courtnee's stall and decided that she was also fun to work with. Besides the over-the-top flirting, the women seemed eager to learn what to do and they were funny as well. Finally, it was Sam's turn. He moved up the barn to where Sam was working.

"Hey, looks like you got the hang of this pretty fast," Alex told her impressed.

"Yeah well, I got lots of practice yesterday," Sam responded, deciding that it didn't matter if she'd done the same thing the day before.

Alex immediately got a frown on his face. "You did this yesterday? I didn't realize—"

Sam cut him off. "It's okay, it's not a big deal. I think I'd rather be doing this than some of the other jobs." She smiled at him to try to let him know that she really was okay with it. "I've never even been near a horse, I'm sure it would buck me off or something."

"Gosh, maybe they should hire you for a permanent job here in the barn," Alex joked.

Sam just looked at him. Was this all he thought she would be good at?

Alex must have noticed that she wasn't laughing.

"Hey, I was kidding," he said. When Sam turned around and continued to clean the stall Alex touched her arm and pulled her around to look at him. "Honestly, I didn't mean anything by it."

Sam shrugged. "It's okay, really."

"Sammi," Alex said, still holding on to her arm, firmly, but not hurting her. "Don't do that."

"Do what?" Sam asked a bit peevishly.

"Don't lie and tell me what you think I want to hear rather than how you really feel." After a beat where Sam didn't say anything, he continued, "If you want to tell me to piss off, tell me. If I do something that hurts your feelings, tell me." His voice suddenly lowered and he took her hands in his. Sam had to lean into him to hear him over the noise of the barn.

"For the love of God, you're the only real person here. If I can't rely on you to tell me like it is, who will?" He paused. "Now, please tell me what upset you."

"It's just that…" She paused, finally continuing when Alex squeezed her hand. "I don't fit in with the other women here, and I don't want you to see me as…less…than they are."

"I don't see you as less," Alex immediately said, not even pausing to think about what he wanted to say. "We don't really know each other, but when I'm lying in my cot at night I find myself thinking about you and what *you* are thinking about." He brushed his knuckle over her reddening cheek and continued, "I'd never intentionally insult you like that. I just have to learn how I can tease you and not have you take offense."

They just stood there and looked at each other for a brief moment until they heard Courtnee laugh in the next stall over. The moment between them was broken and Alex dropped her hands and took a step back.

Searching for something to talk to him about, she asked inanely, "How're you doing? I mean, are you enjoying the experience of dating all these women?"

Alex laughed. "It's certainly interesting."

They spent the next few minutes chatting about nothing in particular while cleaning out one stall and moving on to the next.

Alex rotated between talking with Courtnee, Missy, and Sam for another thirty minutes, then said he had to go and visit with the other women.

"Are you going to miss me?" Missy pouted.

"Uh, yup, but I'll see you later," Alex responded quickly with a look in his eye, like a rabbit cornered by a hound dog.

Missy grabbed Alex and kissed him on the lips, and Courtnee, not to be outdone, also grabbed Alex and kissed her way down his face to his lips. Alex finally extricated himself from the two women and looked toward Sammi. She merely waved at Al from the stall she was cleaning, refusing to stoop to Missy's level of desperation, and then went back to work.

"Whew." Missy fanned her face. "That man is *hot*! I can't wait to have him to myself!"

"What makes you think that'll happen?" Courtnee complained. "There's no guarantee that you'll get the chance."

"You idiot," Missy told Courtnee snidely. "These shows always have one-on-one time with the bachelor. I'll get my chance."

The two women continued to sit on bales of hay and discuss Al and what they'd do when they had him alone and when they won at the end. Sam tuned them out. It was obvious they were pretty much done mucking out the stalls for the day. Figured that as soon as Al left, they stopped pretending and just quit. Sam knew they wouldn't get as many stalls done as they'd done yesterday. After all, it was only her working. She'd do what she could, and Henry would just have to finish up when they were released. She didn't like to put the work back on him, but she could only do so much.

"Hey goodie-two-shoes," Sam heard Courtnee call out and decided to try to ignore her. She wasn't going to start anything with them.

"Hey, I was talking to you!" Sam heard Courtnee say from outside the stall she was currently mucking out.

"What do you want?" Sam asked peevishly, not bothering to even turn and look at the other woman.

"We're going to take a break, we've been working really hard, so you just keep shoveling and make sure you get to the other side of the barn by the time we get back. We wouldn't want anyone to think that you weren't doing your work." Courtnee giggled evilly and turned and left the barn with Missy.

Sam ignored them as they walked out of the barn. It wouldn't do any good to argue, they would do what they wanted to anyway. She'd continue with her work and she'd *not* do theirs as well. It was ridiculous. They were grown women acting like they were in middle school! Sam certainly didn't want to relive middle or high school. It wasn't terrible, but she certainly wasn't one of the popular kids. As a result she occasionally got picked on and teased, but she had a feeling that Courtnee was a pro at making others feel small.

Sam worked hard for the next hour. She'd finished her side of the barn and had even laid down fresh hay. She'd really gotten the hang of the mucking the stalls thing! Since she was finished with her portion of the task, and she was really thirsty, she decided to go around the back of the house where she'd seen a water pump. Perhaps she'd get herself some water. She was hot and tired and she knew she probably smelled horrible.

She walked around the barn to the pump at the back of the house. She didn't see anyone around. Sam pumped some water into her hands and slurped it up. Man, was it good. The water must be coming from deep within the ground because it was ice cold. By the time Sam was finished refreshing herself she was wet from almost head to toe. She'd splashed water onto her face and it had dripped down onto the front of her shirt. She felt much better and could even manage a smile. The water felt so good evaporating from her skin. She turned around to go back to the barn and almost collided with a woman that was standing behind her.

"Oh, excuse me, I didn't see you there," Sam said breathlessly.

"Who are you?" the woman asked with hardly any inflection in her tone.

Sam couldn't tell if she was mad or irritated or some other emotion. She decided it would be best not to antagonize her.

"I'm Sammi," she responded, remembering her "new" name for while she was on the show. "Uh, I was working in the barn and finished up and thought I would come and get a drink…uh…I'm sorry if I'm not supposed to be here, I didn't know."

Nancy looked the woman over. She'd noticed her the day before, but didn't really pay much attention. The woman hadn't done anything to garner any attention. In fact, she couldn't remember what chore she'd been assigned the day before. Nancy noticed that her shirt was about soaked through from the water she'd splashed on her face. Her face was rosy red from the heat and effort she'd been putting forth in the barn. She wasn't as tall as some of the other women, and definitely not as slender, but she wasn't really overweight either. Nancy wasn't even one hundred percent convinced that this woman was even a contestant on the show. She certainly didn't fit the "mold" of the other contestants. Nancy knew she needed to get to know as many of the women as possible if she was going to be able to make an informed choice about who would stay and who would go that day. She went with the assumption that this woman was a contestant.

"It's okay, it *is* a hot day today. I'd rather you drink than pass out from heat exhaustion." And with that she let down the wall she'd unconsciously put up and smiled at Sam. "What are you doing in the barn today? I can only think of one thing, and I'm sure it's not pleasant. What job did you have yesterday?"

Sam smiled at her. "It's not too bad, it's nice to know that what I'm doing will help the horses have a comfortable place to sleep at night. And yesterday I did the same thing! Guess I was really lucky, huh?" she said with a grin.

Nancy couldn't believe that this woman had to muck out the barn twice! The "rules" didn't say anything about having a different job on each day. It was the luck of the draw, she supposed. "Where are you from, Sammi?" Nancy asked.

"Albuquerque, New Mexico. I really like it there. It's not so much a huge city, but it's big enough to have what I want," Sam replied.

"I've never been there," Nancy responded somewhat expectedly, "but I've heard it's a nice city. If you could've done any of the other chores today, what would you have chosen?"

Sam didn't have to think about it and immediately told the woman standing there, "Help with feeding the animals," she responded.

"You sound like you've thought it over. Wouldn't

you want to be in the house where it's air conditioned?" Nancy asked, trying to understand.

"That'd be nice on a day like today," Sam agreed, "but I love animals and I think it would've been interesting to see what everyone eats and how they're all fed," Sammi told her. "I'm a sucker for animals, especially dogs. I have three at home and I'm sure I'd have more if I could. I know that feeding the animals isn't as simple as some people would assume. My dogs all eat the same food, but I have to remember to put Duke's pills in his food, and the supplement in Albert's." Sam winced, it was a bit too much information, she was sure. She continued meekly, trying to forget that she was just babbling on to this stranger. "I would've loved to see the inside of the house, though. I bet it's just as beautiful on the inside as it is on the outside. I love to go to open houses and see all the fancy houses back in Albuquerque. "

Nancy looked at Sam thoughtfully. "Well, I might be biased since I live here, but I sure think it's a beautiful place to live."

"Oh!" Sam exclaimed. "You live here? I'm sorry, I didn't mean to take up your time. I'm sure you're busy. I didn't mean to keep you...I mean...I don't know if I'm even supposed to be talking to you...I'll just be on my way..." Sam looked around as if to see if anyone was seeing what she was going and looked down at her hands. "I'd offer to shake your hand, but I just washed them, and they're still damp and certainly cold."

Nancy smiled at her for the first time. "It's okay, I've shaken cold hands before." And with that she held out her own hand to Sam. Sam didn't really have a choice. She took the woman's hand and shook it firmly. They smiled at each other and each headed back from where they came.

When Nancy reached the house, she looked back to see Sam entering the barn. She tilted her head to the side, nodded, and continued into the house.

Sam entered the barn, and was glad for the shade, even though the smell was pungent. As soon as she shut the barn door she heard Courtnee talking.

"And we were working hard all day and she just walked out and left us to do her part. It's not fair!"

Sam walked up toward the front of the barn and saw Courtnee and Missy talking with John, one of the cowboys who worked on the ranch. Sam hadn't met him face to face, but had seen him from a distance.

"Yeah," Missy joined in. They hadn't seen her standing in the barn door yet. "When we asked where she was going she just glared at us and said 'out.' We couldn't do hers and ours and still get done."

"That's a lie!" Sam said loudly, not able to keep quiet anymore while the women ground her reputation into the dirt at their feet. She startled the trio and they all turned in her direction. "If anyone wasn't doing their parts it was the two of you!"

Courtnee looked Sam up and down, paying attention to her wet shirt and then turned to John and somehow managed to have two tears fall from her eyes. "John, we've been here all day working really hard. Look at our hands, they're filthy!" Missy and Courtnee held out their hands and sure enough they were very dirty. "Let's see *her* hands."

Sam knew this was going to end badly. She knew her hands weren't exactly clean, but they were much cleaner than the other women's since she'd just washed them at the back of the house. She figured the other two women had run their hands through the dirt on the floor recently, just for this reason. Sam hesitated, not knowing whether to show them right away or explain where she was and what she'd been doing. John took the choice out of her hand and didn't let her say a word before saying gruffly, "Let's see 'em."

Sam held out her hands. They were pretty clean as Courtnee accused them of being, albeit covered with calluses and a fresh blister, but clean. The water she'd used to wash them had finally dried.

"Go outside," John said to Missy and Courtnee. The last thing Sam saw was the smirks on their faces as they went out the front of the barn.

"What do you have to say for yourself?" John asked Sam. Sam held up her head. She knew she wouldn't win this and if she tried, it would turn out badly. She now knew what Courtnee and Missy were capable of, and she really didn't want to make a big deal out of this. She knew she was an outsider in the group of women and if she made a misstep she would be even more on the outside.

She took a deep breath and willed the tears gathering in the back of her eyes not to fall and further humiliate her.

"Nothing I think you'd believe," she answered John defiantly.

"I think it's awful that you aren't even trying to do your part," John told her disdainfully. "Everyone else here is out of their element too, but you don't see *them* trying to get out of their work, do you? Look at them,

111

they're all beautiful women who have everything going for them and they're doing their part. I don't know why *you* can't do yours too. You look like you should know better," John said in a scathing tone of voice. He continued, "I expect that the rest of the *ladies* will be done with their chores soon, but since you decided you didn't want to do yours, you can finish up in here. It looks like there are ten stalls left. You clean those out and put down fresh straw. Once you finish that you can come back and join the others. If there's time left you can eat your lunch late, which is what everyone else will be doing while you're doing the work that you should've done earlier today. I'll inspect your work before you'll be allowed to leave, so don't think you can somehow get out of it. Everyone on this ranch does their part. We don't tolerate those who don't pull their own weight." And with that John left the barn.

Sam took another deep breath and couldn't keep a few tears from squeezing out of her eyes. She was exhausted. She'd already cleaned out most of the other stalls that day. She figured she'd do more in the first place since she knew Missy and Courtnee had no clue what they were doing and she figured they'd slack off. It wasn't fair to the horses to come back to a messy stall just because she didn't want to do extra. Besides, she really didn't have a choice. What the hell was she doing here? This was one more thing that made her think it was time for her to go home. No one wanted her here, so why was she still trying to participate in this stupid show? Sam picked up the pitchfork, walked to the first stall and tried to forget how good looking Al was and how she felt when he singled her out to talk to.

The women were all gathered around the buffet table that had been set out on the expansive lawn of the ranch. Discussions were going back and forth about the day and about the adventures the women had. Jennie and Kiki were telling everyone they'd made most of the meal. They were very proud of themselves. They acted like they made the entire meal all by themselves, when most of the women knew that certainly wasn't the case. They were all pretty tired from their chores for the day and for the most part took their seats on the long picnic tables and ate. There weren't even that many comments about how many calories they were consuming, they were just too tired to think about it.

Alex had spent the day going from chore to chore, talking with the women and trying to get to know them all a bit better. It was tough, especially when they were competing for his attention. That was something he usually laughed about and enjoyed when he was out with his buddies, but for some reason it was grating on his nerves here. He went in the house to look for Aunt Nancy so they could go over the highlights of the day on the tapes.

Alex found Nancy in the back family room. It looked like she'd gotten a head start and was watching the tapes from the chores from earlier in the day. She was taking it very seriously. She had a notepad out and was taking notes about the women and their actions. Al smiled. He'd always liked his aunt and he was sorry they didn't get to see each other that much since they lived on different continents.

"How's it goin'?" Alex asked her.

"Hummm," she responded, not really paying him

113

any attention.

Alex laughed. "That good, huh? What do you think?"

Nancy turned her head and looked her nephew in the eye. "What I've noticed is that they were all on their best behavior when you were with them, and when you left their real personalities came out," she told him honestly.

"I expected as much," Alex replied. "Who's on the top of your list to go today?"

"I still think I'm leaning toward Candi and Katie. They seem to be the ones that do the least work and want the most attention. They wouldn't last very long at your ranch. It's too far out and there isn't enough attention there for them."

"Who do you like the most?" Alex asked his aunt. Since she knew who she thought should go first, he wanted her honest opinion on the other women. At some point he was going to have to choose one to keep at the end of the show. "Does anyone stand out?"

Nancy pressed the pause button on the television and looked at Alex. "It's hard to say, really. I don't really know them all that well, and it's hard to tell from meeting them on such short notice."

Alex interrupted, "That's what I've been going through. I tried to tell you."

"Don't be cheeky," Nancy replied, "there are a few I do like. I met that Sammi woman today. Did you know that she had to muck out the barn two days in a row? I wouldn't wish that on my worst enemy. Even the ranch hands switch out that duty."

"Yeah, I hadn't realized it until today when I was helping them. That's definitely one of the worst jobs the women had to do today. All three were doing a good job when I left, though. Where did you meet Sammi? Don't tell me you took a trip down to the barn?" Alex asked his aunt with an arch of his brow.

"Don't be absurd! Of course not. She came up to the water pump to get a drink and cool off," Nancy replied. "We had a short conversation and she went back to the barn."

"Who else do you like?" Alex asked, trying to get the conversation off of Sammi. He wasn't ready to admit to his aunt how much he was attracted to Sammi.

"Amy seems to be nice, as well as Kathi and Ashley," Nancy told him.

"That's about what I think too," Alex said, again downplaying his own thoughts about Sammi and the other women. "Let's finish watching this and let Eddie know who the pick is and we'll get out of your hair. I'm sure you'll be glad to have your house back."

The two sat and watched the rest of the tapes, laughing at the antics of the women trying to get and hold his attention. It was obvious they were all out of their element, but most were genuinely trying to do their chores. Finally, Nancy made her decision. It'd been a long day and it was time to have the ceremony so the women could go back to their camp and Alex and the producers could get back to theirs to start editing the tapes.

Susan Stoker

Chapter Thirteen

Alex and his aunt strolled out to the porch to see the women were done eating and were sitting around chatting. The food had been taken away and it seemed as if they were just waiting on the camera crews and the producers to set them up for the final shot of the day. Alex saw Sammi walk over from the direction of the barn. Her shoulders were dropping and she looked dejected or exhausted or something. She didn't look up as she walked, but instead stared at the ground as if it was the most fascinating thing she'd ever seen. Alex couldn't understand what she was doing…did she go back to the barn after she ate? Something was going on and he didn't know what it was. He hated that. There wasn't any food left out, it had been taken away about half an hour ago. Had she taken another walk? If so, why did she look so depressed and defeated? He watched her to go the end of one of the long picnic tables, sit, put her head down on her arms and go still. Alex looked at his aunt as if to ask if she had seen Sammi's actions, but her attention was on one of the ranch hands, John, who was walking toward them.

"Ma'am, if I may have a word with you, please," John asked Nancy in a grave tone of voice.

"Of course, John," she replied.

John looked at Alex as if to ask Nancy if they could go somewhere private

"Alex is my nephew, I don't have any secrets from him, go ahead," Nancy told him.

John shrugged and continued, "I was checking on

the ladies who were working in the barn and it seems we had a problem, but I took care of it."

"I can't imagine what kind of problem you're talking about. The women weren't expected to be perfect at their jobs, what's the issue?" she asked him with genuine bafflement.

"When I got there to check the work there were only two women working. They told me that the third hadn't done much work that day and that they had to do more than their fair share of the stalls. While we were talking the third came in and contradicted the others' stories. I looked at their hands. The two women who were there had real dirty workin' hands and the third didn't have any dirt on her hands at all! So to make sure that everything was fair I had the third stay and finish up the barn. I just thought you should know. I checked her work and it was fine. The horses will be in clean stalls tonight, just like every night. I wanted to put your mind at ease. I also wanted to let you know what happened in case she tried to come complain to you…or to you," he said, looking at Alex.

"John, are you sure that you took the time to read the situation right? If the third person is who I think it was, I met her at the water pump and she told me she'd just finished her stalls and was taking a break, washing her hands and her face and getting a drink of water," Nancy questioned John carefully.

"Um, well, it seemed to be the right decision at the time," John stuttered, not knowing what to think.

Alex was furious. He could just imagine what had happened. Missy and Courtnee had taken advantage of the fact that Sammi wasn't there when John came in to check on their work and took credit for what she'd done. When she walked in the barn with clean hands John jumped to the obvious conclusion. They were all working when he was there with them, but he knew that many of the women changed after he'd left their sight. He thought he knew Sammi pretty well, especially after watching her not complain about the treatment she'd received from some of the women in camp as well her lack of complaints when she was injured or uncomfortable.

"I'm not sure what happened, John, but I'll find out, you can go. If I find that you misjudged that woman you *will* apologize to her *and* be on stall duty for the rest of the week," Nancy told him sternly.

John looked a little sheepish but said, "Yes, ma'am," and headed for the bunkhouse.

Nancy looked at Alex, who looked ready to explode.

"Calm down, Alex, let me handle this," Nancy told him sternly. "I don't believe that's what really happened either, but I won't take the empowerment away from my ranch hands either."

They both looked over at the tables. Sammi hadn't moved. She was in the same position as a few minutes ago. Head on her arms on the table. Since the production crew was still setting up for the final scene of the day Nancy sent one of the kitchen staff over to get Sammi and told her to bring her to the front room in the house. They watched as the girl bent over Sammi, touched her shoulder, then finally shook her gently. Sammi lifted her head at the summons, then looked at the house and nodded to the girl. She slowly got up and headed for the front door.

"What'd ya do now, Miss Bitch?" Courtnee yelled

out as Sammi shuffled past. "Getting called to the principal's office because you didn't do your work?" And with that she and several other women laughed.

Sam glared at Courtnee and said, "You should know." She kept walking. It wasn't worth it to continue to try to come up with a comeback that was better than that. She was beyond tired and every muscle in her body hurt.

Sam was surprised when she was asked to come up to the house. She figured it couldn't get any worse than the cowboy looking disdainfully at her and determining that her work in the barn was just "okay." Damn it, she'd cleaned the entire barn by herself. Well, almost the entire barn, Missy and Courtnee had worked when Al had been there. Sam laughed at herself, well, she'd wanted to get a look inside the house and she guessed she was now getting her chance.

Sam was led into the front room and stopped short. The woman she'd met earlier that day was there, along with Al. "Shit," Sam muttered to herself. She wasn't sure whether she was supposed to stay standing or sit down…but she also wasn't completely confident that she'd be able to stand there without falling over, but she'd do it or die trying. She was embarrassed enough having to be there in front of the woman and Al like a naughty child. She wasn't going to fall over, no matter what…maybe.

"Sit down, Sammi," Nancy said, motioning toward a chair in front of the large desk.

Sam hesitated for half a second before deciding that she'd better sit just so there was no chance she would fall flat on her face. She gratefully sat, back ramrod straight looking only at the woman. She definitely didn't want to look at Al. This was too humiliating. Some impression she was making. Maybe they were going to tell her that she was going home right this minute. Was that it? That had to be it. But she didn't see Eddie or Robert talking to the woman, although she'd seen the cowboy from the barn talking to Nancy and saw Al's frown. This wasn't going to be a fun interview, she was sure of it.

"Sammi," Nancy began, "my ranch hand told me quite a story about what happened in the barn today. Would you like to me tell your side of what happened?"

Sam looked at Nancy, then dared to glance at Al. He was standing with his arms crossed in front of him with a stern look on his face. There was no way that Sam was going to rat out the other women. They were already making her life miserable. There was no telling what would happen if she made them be caught in a lie.

"No, ma'am," Sam told the woman.

Nancy raised her eyebrows and said incredulously, "Nothing? So you admit that you did nothing all day while the other women did all the work while you were just lounging around? You only worked when Al was there but stopped when he left? Is that right?" Nancy asked, deliberately trying to get under the young woman's skin.

"Ma'am, John made a judgment call based on the facts he received. I can't fault him for that. I willingly accepted my punishment. You'll find that your horses will be able to rest peacefully tonight in clean beds. That really should be all you care about. Not who did what. The chore was completed. You'll never see me again after today," Sammi responded in a dull voice.

"Damn it, Sammi," Alex started to say.

"No," Sammi interrupted. "Neither of you were there and you have to trust your employees." She looked Nancy in the eyes and continued, "You can't go around second guessing decisions that are made around here. It's a simple business decision. You empower your employees to make decisions and you stand behind them when they do, whether they are wrong or right. If they are wrong you discuss what happened and talk about what might be done differently the next time. John did what he thought was right. I accepted it, end of story."

The three of them sat there, looking at each other for a long moment. Finally, Nancy broke the silence, "I'm fairly certain you weren't at fault today. I saw you at the pump, I know you were covered with dirt and who knows what else when you got there and that you cleaned yourself up. I do trust my employees, but I also don't like for anyone to get blamed and/or punished for something they didn't do. Should I bring John in here to tell his side of the story again to see if we can't get to the bottom of this?" Nancy asked in a hard voice.

Sam sighed. She'd screwed up and obviously pissed off the woman in front of her. The last thing she wanted to do was get someone else in trouble for her stupidity. She should've known that Courtnee would pull something. All in all it wasn't that big of a deal. This was a stupid television show after all. Suddenly remembering Robert and the show, Sam looked around. She didn't see any cameras...which was odd. "Where are the cameras?" she asked belatedly, more to

herself than actually thinking that anyone would
answer.

"This is a ranch matter, not one for television,"
Nancy told her with crisp intonation. "Do you want me
to get John in here?" she asked again, not letting
Sammi leave the question unanswered.

"No," Sam said, sharper than she intended. She
tried to calm herself down and said in a gentler voice,
"Look, I'll apologize to whomever you want me to. I
took responsibility for what happened today. I'm sorry,
it won't happen again." She laughed a bit at that and
continued, "Not that I'll have the chance to do it
again." She stopped laughing and looked the woman in
the eyes and said earnestly, "I believe I did the best I
could in that barn. John did the right thing, the only
thing he could, and I probably would've done the same
thing he did in the same situation. The evidence was
against me and I took the punishment. Can I go? I'm
sure the producers are ready to start by now." She
finished lamely and desperately.

Nancy and Alex looked at each other and Alex
gave her a curt nod.

"Fine, you can go. But Sammi," Nancy said as
Sam shakily stood up and started for the door, "not
everyone is so easily fooled. Get some rest."

Sam paused at the door and turned back to Nancy
with a small smile. Even with everything that was said
and the position that she was in she couldn't resist
saying, "I was right, it *is* just as beautiful as the
outside," and she walked out the door.

"What was that about?" Alex asked his aunt,
baffled by Sammi's last comment.

"Never mind about that," Nancy said gruffly but

with a trace of a smile. "What do you think?" she asked her nephew seriously.

"I don't know who or what she's protecting, but it's damn annoying. We both know she wouldn't have shirked her duty. Why won't she tell us what really happened?" Alex asked his aunt.

"I'm not sure, but she has nerves of steel. She was ready to fall over, but it looked like sheer stubbornness was keeping her upright," Nancy said thoughtfully. "I like her."

Alex looked at his aunt. "So do I," he said solemnly.

* * *

Sam walked back out to the yard. *All I have to do is get through this so I can go back to the camp and get some sleep.* Her hands hurt. Her back hurt. Her legs hurt. Hell, there wasn't a body part that didn't hurt, but underneath the hurt she felt strangely good. She'd done a great job today, and no one would be able to take that pride away from her.

It seemed as if Eddie and the other producers and Robert were finally ready for the "vote off," as Sam started calling it. She was fairly certain she might be the one going home. There was no telling who else Missy and Courtnee had spewed their story to. If it was Eddie, he might make her go home for not fulfilling the rules of the show or something. All she could do was wait along with everyone else. At this point she almost didn't care. Almost.

Sam watched as Al took his spot next to Robert. He looked good. He looked more rugged now than he had before. Sam figured it was because he'd been outside most of the day and doing all the chores. She really couldn't see him doing the laundry or mopping the floor, but she'd heard snippets of the other women's conversations who'd claimed he'd done just that.

Robert was making his speech about what a great job they'd all done that day and how he was impressed with their work ethics. He asked if there were any comments about the day. A few women spoke, but for the most part it seemed that they were just as anxious to get this over with as Sam was. Blessedly, even Missy and Courtnee kept their mouths shut. *Maybe they figured the less people they tell their lies to the more likely they will get away with it.* Sam thought. Finally, Robert was getting to the "vote off."

"As you know, ladies, one of you must be going home today. We know it's been a long day and you are tired. No one wants to leave this beautiful country and miss out on the company of Al, but alas, it must be done." Sam didn't think that Robert sounded very remorseful.

He continued with his grand speech, "There were many factors that were taken into account on who'd be leaving today. It wasn't only one thing that sealed her fate, but a multitude of factors. To keep you on your toes, those factors will not be revealed to you. The person who will be leaving today is…" Robert paused to get the most dramatic effect out of his audience… "Katie."

Sam let out a breath she wasn't even aware she'd been holding. She'd thought for sure that her time was up. Katie cried and hugged some of the other women she'd gotten to know on the show. She walked up to where Al and Robert were standing. Al led her away to the waiting car to say goodbye.

"It's time to go back to camp, ladies," Robert told them. "Please gather up your belongings and say goodbye and we'll go."

Since Al was walking back to the group most of the women walked toward him to say their *personal* goodbyes for the day. Sam went to sit at one of the tables until they had to load up the bus. As she was walking toward a table she saw Henry approaching her. Sam veered a bit to meet him. She'd liked the gruff cowboy. He'd made the first day of mucking out the stables pretty fun. Sam put her hands in her back pockets as they approached each other.

"Hey, Sammi!" Henry said with a drawl. "You look like shit," he continued with no remorse.

Sam laughed as she was sure he meant her to. "Thanks, you sure know how to soothe my ego a bit."

"No, really, you look worn to the bone. What time you finished up today?" he asked her.

"You'll never guess." Sammi grinned up at him, avoiding directly answering his question.

Henry raised his brows while waiting expectantly for her to answer.

"Let's just say I'm starving because I didn't make dinner," Sam told him with a grin, not about to go into the details about why she hadn't gotten to eat.

Henry put his head back and laughed. "Damn, that's bad luck! Why'd it take so long?"

Sam's smile dimmed a bit. Not wanting to answer him, she skirted around his question and instead simply said, "I'll be glad not to see another barn for a while."

She ran her hand through her hair, brushing it back off her face.

Henry suddenly reached out and grabbed her wrist.

"Wha…" Sam got out as she flinched in surprise. What did she really know about this cowboy after all?

Alex watched Sammi out of the corner of his eye as the other women said their goodbyes. He didn't know why it bothered him to see her smile at one of the cowboys, but he knew he was irritated. His mood only grew worse when he saw the cowboy throw his head back and laugh at something Sammi said. He'd just finished saying the correct meaningless goodbye words to Kiki when he saw the ranch hand grab Sammi by the wrist. Without a second thought he was striding across the yard to where Sammi stood.

"What in the hell did you do?!?" Henry rasped as he turned Sam's hand over to look at her palm. Sam tried to tug her hand away from him.

"Let me go," Sam said firmly. Henry gripped her wrist even more firmly.

"Not until you explain this," Henry said gruffly, trying to pull her toward him so he could get a better look at her palm.

"She said to let go of her," a deep voice said from behind them. Henry dropped her hand and they both turned to see Alex standing a few feet from them.

"You okay?" he asked Sam, shifting so his body was between her and the cowboy. Alex didn't know what was going on, but he wasn't going to allow this guy to touch her without her permission again. Alex didn't even take the time to think about what he just thought. He'd never been the possessive, alpha type, but Sammi somehow brought it out in him.

Sam tucked her hand back in her jeans pocket and said, "Yup, I've got to get on the bus..."

"You won't until I find out what the hell just happened here," Alex told her with a glare. He turned his eyes to Henry. "If you want to keep your job you'd better start explaining."

Henry answered immediately and calmly, "She's hurt, I was trying to look at her hand." He'd seen Alex around a bit and knew that his bark was worse than his bite. Suppressing a smile, knowing that this woman seemed to have gotten under his skin, he nodded at Sam and said, "Look for yourself."

Both men turned to see Sam backing away from them, hands still out of sight. "They're all waiting for me...I have to go," she stammered, almost tripping over herself trying to get away. "It was nice to meet you, Henry," Sam said, still backing away.

Alex came toward her as if he was a predator stalking his prey. "Give me your hand," he ordered, holding out his own.

"It's not a big deal, Al," Sam tried to explain, "it's just a blister from working today, I'm sure that all the others have them too..."

Alex stepped close enough to take her by the upper arm and stop her retreat.

"It's a bit more than that, hon," Henry said. "I'll leave you to deal with her," he told Al as he turned around to go back to the barn.

"Damn," Sam muttered under her breath, not believing how Henry had thrown her under the proverbial bus when it came to Alex.

"You know you're going to make my life

miserable by giving me this attention, don't you?" Sam tried to reason with Alex. "They're okay, it's not life threatening. Just let me go…please?"

"I can't let you go knowing that you might be hurt," Alex told her honestly. "What kind of man would I be if I just let you walk away right now knowing you were in pain and I didn't do anything about it?" Alex stared into Sammi's eyes, trying desperately to make her understand that he wanted to help her, that he *needed* to help her.

Sam somehow knew he'd stand there all night waiting if she didn't just get it over with and show him. She pulled out her left hand, knowing it wasn't as bad as the right one.

"Fine, you want to see it, here," and with that she shoved it under his face.

"Holy shit, Sammi," Alex muttered, rubbing his thumb over the back of her hand while holding her palm up. It didn't look good. There were blisters on the palm under each finger. She had what looked like a blister on top of a blister at the base of her thumb and one large blister right in the center of her palm.

"What the hell happened? Why didn't you use gloves?" Alex practically yelled at her, not able to hold back his concern about how she was hurt. While he sounded mad, the hand that was holding hers was gentle.

Sam tried to yank her hand away from him, but he held firm.

"I couldn't find them this afternoon and I had to get the job done, so I did it. It's not a big deal, Al. Really. *Please*, let me get on the bus, they're all looking at us," Sam said desperately. As much as she

129

loved the feel of Al's hands on hers she knew she'd pay for it. If she thought Courtnee and the others were playing the game before, they would really start on her now. She was enemy number one in every way.

"Let me see the other one," Alex said remorselessly, not giving into her pleas until he'd seen for himself how badly she was hurt.

Sam sighed. She knew he wouldn't let her go until he'd seen the other hand as well. Reluctantly, she pulled it out of her pocket and held it out.

Alex didn't say a word, just took a hold of her right hand and held it close to his face to get a better look. It was a bit worse than the other one since she was right handed. Some of the blisters were really oozing and looked like they needed to be cleaned.

"Let's go," Alex told her abruptly, trying to tow her toward the big house.

"Where?" Sam asked, trying to pull back in the direction of the bus.

"To the house where we can have that looked at by a doctor," Alex answered determinately.

"No way!" Sam said, yanking her hand out of his grasp and taking a large step backward and away from him. "I'm going back to the bus and leaving right now. I'll clean it back at camp," she promised somewhat desperately.

Alex looked at her, then back to the bus. "Okay, I can understand you wouldn't want the other women to think you were getting unfair attention from me, but you have to have this taken care of. It won't wait."

Sam sighed and asked, "Can we compromise? Can Eddie have one of his people look at it back at camp?"

Alex pondered her statement, not liking the entire

situation at all. He wanted to be the one to take care of her. He wanted to be the one who made her feel better. He really wanted her to lean on him and to see him as able to take care of her. This situation was so messed up. There was no way in the "real world" that he'd let her just go off into the night knowing that she needed care. He sighed and finally said, "Okay, but the next time we get together I want to see for myself that they are healing. And know that if we weren't on this show I'd take you in and make sure you were cared for. I'd probably draw you a hot bubble bath, cook you a comforting dinner and make sure you took care of yourself. I have a feeling you take care of others more than you take care of yourself."

Sam couldn't say anything at first. She allowed her eyes to say what her heart felt. She'd never had someone take care of her like that and there was nothing she wanted more than to let Al take care of her. But she knew she couldn't, and for her own self-preservation she had to get on that bus right now and get away from the most handsome and caring man she's ever met. She gave him a wistful but honest, smile and softly said, "Deal." Then she turned her back on Al and walked toward the bus.

Alex watched her go. He was pleased at the smile she'd bestowed on him. It lit up her face and was definitely not the kind of smile he was used to seeing on women. He was used to seeing a small fake curling of the lips, seldom did the women he was around show any teeth when they smiled. It was refreshing to see an unfettered smile, aimed at him. Alex turned away to talk to Eddie before he left the ranch. He wanted to see the tapes from the doctor looking at her hands later that night. He just couldn't let it go. He had to see for himself that she was taken care of. It was a compulsion of sorts, and he really wasn't very happy about it.

The bus was quiet on the way back to the camp. Sam fell asleep in the front seat as soon as they left the ranch. When they pulled up to the camp it almost seemed as if they were back home, as much of a "home" it could be. Eddie had obviously sent one of the camp doctors to meet the bus as there was a man in a white coat waiting when the bus pulled up. He called Sam over and had her sit on the truck bed he'd driven to the camp while he doctored her hands. It hurt, but Sam was so tired it wasn't as bad as it could've been. The doctor bandaged up her hands and was on his way. He didn't say much to her. Sam figured it was back to the "show" rules, but he did tell her to keep her hands dry that night and that they should be bandaged each night and covered with the salve to keep them moist and to help them heal.

Sam went into the tent to lie down. She figured that a shower could wait. Even though she was filthy, she couldn't imagine being able to stand up for the amount of time that it would take. Besides, the doctor told her to keep her hands dry. The other women slowly filed into the tent after visiting the bathroom and shower.

Kathi came to stand near Sam's cot and said nastily, "So, did you plan that little interlude or what? You think you can outsmart us to get to spend more time with Al? Ain't gonna happen, bitch. You don't have a shot in hell at that man. Look at you, you're pathetic. Your games aren't going to work."

Sam looked up at Kathi and said quietly and

honestly, "That wasn't what I was trying to do. All I wanted was to leave. He was the one who insisted that he look at my hands. I don't figure that I am going to win this game either."

"Damn straight," piped up Cindee. By now most of the women who were living in the tent had wandered over.

"It seems to me that Al is the kind of man who would care about anyone that was hurt," Sam continued. "It wasn't as if he was showing me any extra affection or consideration. He would have done the same thing if it'd been one of you that was hurt." Sam looked at each woman. "Look at it this way, now that my hands aren't in top shape that leaves me more vulnerable to not being able to succeed in the future challenges!"

The girls laughed.

"That's true," said Brandi.

They slowly all went back to their beds. It'd been a long two days and most of them were ready to get some sleep. Kathi was the last one standing near Sam's bed.

"You might have fooled them," she said in a low furious voice, cocking her head toward the other women settling down into their beds for the night, "but Missy and Courtnee told me what you did today. You like to make others think you're a saint, but you and I both know better. If you think he likes to help women that are hurt feel better, you'd better not egg him on."

Sam sighed and looked at Kathi. "Go to bed Kathi, I'm not going to fight with you. Did you see me cozying up to him? Did you see me go to him first? No. I wasn't even going to tell him, so there's fault in

your logic. Remember too that this whole thing is
Courtnee and Missy's fault. If they hadn't lied, I
wouldn't have been hurt in the first place and Al
wouldn't have had to be concerned about me. I don't
need him or any man to help me feel better, I can do it
myself. Don't mess with me, Kathi. I'll stay out of
your way and you stay out of mine. We only have to be
around each other for another week or two and then we
won't ever have to see each other again."

"I can't wait," Kathi hissed and walked away.

Sam sighed. This wasn't going well. She sure
hoped that the next week or two passed quickly, or that
she was taken out of the show before things got really
ugly.

* * *

Alex didn't go straight back to the camp. He
stayed back at the ranch to visit with his aunt Nancy
for a bit. He wasn't sure when he'd get to see her again
and he missed her. They talked a little about what had
happened that night. Neither could understand what
was going through Sammi's head, and while they had a
good idea about what went on in the barn, neither
knew for sure. When Alex asked the producer about
tapes from the barn, he'd told them that the cameras
had taped them while he was helping them out and
stayed for a bit afterward, but hadn't been back. That
wasn't going to help them figure out what happened.

"You said her hands had blisters all over them?"
Nancy asked her nephew with concern in her voice.

"Yes, and they were bad. I don't know how she
was able to muck the barn out with them like that,"

Alex told her, still beyond concerned about if she'd gotten help when she got back to her camp.

"I'm sure they were fine when she was up at the water pump," Nancy told him. "We shook hands and I didn't see her flinch or feel anything out of the ordinary. In fact, I was impressed that she actually shook my hand and didn't give me a "limp fish" handshake. She couldn't have done that if she'd been hurt then."

Alex agreed with his aunt. "She must not have used gloves when she went back to the barn. We could ask John about it," Alex told her, getting ready to stand up to go and find John right that second. Anything to help get to the bottom of what happened. He was having a hard time letting it go.

"Let's just forget about it. We don't know what happened, but it doesn't really matter now. Sammi was right, John made a judgment call. We might not like it, but we weren't there either. She seems to be okay, tired but fine." Trying to change the subject, Nancy said, "Let's talk about what they have planned for you for the upcoming week," Nancy told him, settling in to speculate about what was going to happen next on the show.

Alex and Nancy spent the next couple of hours catching up and talking about the show and the ladies. Soon it was time for Alex to get back to the camp. He was anxious to see the tapes and see how Sammi's hands were.

Alex sat in his tent with the tapes from that night. He was told that all the women were sound asleep or at least in the tents for the night. He watched as the doctor cleaned and bandaged Sammi's hands. Neither

said much. Alex could tell that the cleansing process
was hurting her. He could see her biting her bottom lip,
but she didn't say a word. He watched as Sammi
walked back to her tent. Eddie had also given him
another tape. It was one from the inside of one of the
women's tents. They knew that these cameras were
there, it was all a part of the show.

Alex watched as the women settled down and got
ready for bed. This camera was more of a "wide angle"
lens, so he didn't have any close up shots of anyone,
but he saw Kathi walk up to Sammi's bed as she was
lying on it. He heard bits and pieces of the
conversation, enough to know that Kathi was giving
Sammi a hard time about the attention he'd given her.

That's what she was talking about. Alex thought
to himself. No wonder she just wanted me to leave her
alone.

Alex watched as the other women gathered around
to hear the conversation. Alex was amazed to hear
Sammi peg him when she was defending his gallant
tendencies and explain how he didn't like to see
women hurt. He was surprised she knew that about
him already. They really hadn't spent that much time
together, but he'd hoped that perhaps she had some
feelings toward him. Hearing her defend him made
him realize their attraction wasn't just on his side. It
made him smile.

Alex watched the conversation and saw the
women drift off toward their own beds until it was
only Kathi and Sammi left talking. He saw Kathi lean
in toward Sammi. He couldn't hear what she was
saying, the camera only picked up bits and pieces of
the conversation.

I'll have to tell Eddie to turn up the microphone.
Alex thought as he strained to hear what was being said. He heard Kathi say something like, "saint, help women, and egg." Alex wasn't sure what to make of that. He couldn't hear what Sammi said in response, but as she spoke her words got louder and he was able to hear the end of the conversation.

"I don't *need* him or any man to help me feel better, I can do it myself." He chuckled to himself. Alex never thought he could be attracted to an *independent* woman, but he found he liked the thought of Sammi not needing him, but perhaps wanting him instead. Lord knew that he wanted her. He was attracted to her. More than attracted. He was thrilled that there was at least some reciprocation on Sammi's behalf.

Alex watched as Kathi stormed back to her bed. He was definitely glad for the opportunity to watch the tapes from camp. He was learning a lot about the personalities of the women, and what he was learning made him more and more cynical. He was amazed at how different the ladies were around him than they were around each other. He shuddered to think about having to make a decision without knowing the true personalities of the women. Thank God he was able to see the tapes. It was bad enough to feel like a piece of meat that dogs were fighting over.

He felt as if with the tapes at least he could have a fighting chance of making the right decision at the end of the show. He might not like Eddie very much as a person, but as a producer he certainly knew how to make a show exciting.

Susan Stoker

Chapter Fourteen

The next week went by fairly quickly for Sam. Her hands healed quickly, enough so that it no longer hurt to use them. Al was true to his word and checked them himself the first time they saw each other after the incident. It should have been awkward since they were still basically strangers, but instead it was awkward for Sam because of how she felt when Al had taken her hands in his and run his fingertips over her quickly healing palms.

Sam wanted to grab him and never let go. She imagined those hands running over the rest of her body and it was all she could do to not fall in a puddle at his feet.

The days at camp were lazy ones. Sam no longer took walks away from the camp, not because she didn't want to, but because she didn't want to put any of the camera operators in danger again. She still blamed herself for Kina almost being bitten and didn't want to have a repeat.

The women went through challenges and won "prizes" such as small group dates with Al and even a visit to a hot spring to soak in the soothing waters. There were four more women who'd been "voted off"—Candi, Nikki, Brandi, and Jennie. The women came back to camp after Jennie had left to find that one of the bunkhouses had disappeared and they'd all be staying in one. That was a tough adjustment for most of the women because they'd gotten used to the space and only having four or five of them in each

139

bunkhouse.

Sam was surprised that she was still around. For the most part she avoided Kathi, Courtnee, and Missy. They certainly weren't friends, but at least they weren't enemies either. Apparently the last run in with Kathi and the threats that hung in the air between them was enough to chill Kathi out. Sam hung out mostly with Amy and Lori. They didn't have much in common, but when a person is put in a situation where there isn't much to do, comradeship is forced.

The women who were left were Ashley from Toledo, Cindee from Albany, Lori from Colorado Springs, Kiki from Miami, Courtnee from Pensacola, Missy from LA, Amy from El Paso, Kathi from Knoxville, and Sammi. It was an interesting mix of women. There were definitely cliques that had formed. Kathi, Courtnee, Missy, and Kiki had banded together. They acted like they were the "popular" girls in high school. They sat together, got ready in the mornings together, and probably most importantly, they helped each other in the challenges. That wasn't exactly illegal, but it reminded Sam of the Alliances that were formed in the game of Survivor.

Today was a big day because the prize for being in the top three of today's challenge was a one-on-one date with Al. So far in the show there hadn't been any of those types of dates. They'd all either been the entire group together or four or five of them at a time. They were all hoping to win one of these dates, but Sam knew that the "Clique" would do everything in their power to win. Sam hoped, however, that since there were four of them and only three slots for the individual dates that could work against them and their so-called friendship might not be able to handle that type of competition.

The nine women were told to wear their bathing suits and to be on the bus by nine in the morning. Obviously this was going to be a water completion. Sam was nervous, while she had a pretty healthy body image, there was no way she'd be able to compete with the other women. She was heavier than them, and she knew if she had to stand next to them while they were all wearing their skimpy swimsuits that she'd definitely be at a disadvantage.

The bus pulled out at precisely nine in the morning. The bus ride turned out to be one of the longest they'd been on to get to a challenge so far. Sam suspected it was because they had to drive away to get to a body of water. Finally they pulled up to the most beautiful lake Sam had ever seen. It was crystal clear and huge. The production staff had obviously gotten there quite a bit earlier because they had all the cameras set up. There was what looked like an obstacle course set up in the water. Sam smiled to herself. If this was a water swimming challenge, she was set.

They piled out of the bus and went to stand in front of Robert, who of course, looked immaculate. Courtnee and Missy had already taken off their tops and were wearing shorts and a bikini top. Al looked gorgeous as usual. He was wearing his usual blue jeans but had substituted his button up shirt for a white T-shirt.

Sam tried to covertly look at Al. Over the last week she'd gotten to know him a little better. She hadn't had any time alone with him, but she honestly thought they were clicking. Of course, every time she thought she'd see one of the other women plastered all over him, she'd have to give herself a mental smack in the head She thought they were clicking…that was what he was supposed to do with every contestant. They were all supposed to feel like they were the "one" for him.

Sam, Beth, and Christina had had a long conversation about this before she left for the Outback. Every time they watched a reality show they'd laughed at how emotional the women were and wondered how in the world anyone could say they were in love with someone who their whole relationship with was in front of a camera and therefore probably fake. But she got it now. It was a very intense atmosphere. There were no other distractions. The only focus was on the other person. It made for an intimate setting, manufactured, but intimate nonetheless. Sam was brought out of her musings when she heard Robert start talking.

"Welcome, ladies!" Robert boomed once everyone was in place and the cameras were rolling. "Today, you'll be competing against each other for a one-on-one date with Al. The three women who finish the course the fastest will each get to spend half a day with Al on a date of his choice. Here are the rules. Each of you will be going through the course individually. You'll enter the lake here, swim to the first buoy...attached to the buoy at the end of a rope is a small weight. You'll need to swim down to the end of the rope and untie the weight and let it fall. Then you are to swim to the next buoy and untie the weight at the end of the rope that's hanging from that rope. You will continue around the buoys until you have untied all the weights. The weight on each rope gets heavier and heavier as well as deeper and deeper as you swim around. You will then swim back to the starting point and once you cross the finish line your time will stop. The three women who either finish the course the fastest or go the furthest in the shortest amount of time will win the one-on-one dates with Al. Are there any questions?"

The contestants were given time to examine the course from the shore. On TV it always seemed as if the people just went right onto the game, but in reality that wasn't the case. There was an obnoxious amount of time spent on safety talks and explaining over and over how it was done. One of the producers even demonstrated the entire course so they would understand what they needed to do and wouldn't screw it up once they were on camera. It was exhausting and exasperating. Sam just wanted to get started already.

Once they were ready to start, Cindee asked what order they'd be competing in and Robert told her that Al would be pulling their names out of a hat to see the order they would go in. Sam almost laughed out loud. This competition had her name written all over it. She knew she could easily beat most, if not all, of the women. She hadn't been on her state champion winning water polo for nothing! Al pulled the names out of the hat and as luck would have it, Sam's name was chosen eighth. Kathi's was chosen to go last.

Sam felt way too giddy about being able to spend some time with Al alone. She again tried to warn herself that what she was feeling was manufactured and in no way could be real, but she couldn't help herself. Al was hot, and she had a major crush on him.

143

Every time she felt his eyes on her she daydreamed that maybe, just maybe, he was feeling the same way about her.

First up was Courtnee. Since she already had her top off, she slowly shimmied out of her shorts, leaving her standing in nothing but a skimpy black bikini. Sam groaned softly. It didn't look like there was an ounce of fat on her. Her legs were long and lean, her boobs big, but not too big. Basically, she was perfect. The camera operators were getting close up shots of her body as she sauntered to the starting line. Hell, even her ass didn't jiggle! Al was standing by the lake to wish each of them well before they started. Sam and the other women couldn't hear what was being said, but by Courtnee's body language they could tell that whatever he was saying to her was quite intimate.

The producers put up a set of bleachers for the women to sit on while they were waiting their turns. They watched as Courtnee went into the water and started paddling toward the first buoy. The distances weren't that far, maybe seventy-five yards, but it looked like Courtnee was struggling before she even got to the first buoy. She was doing a kind of dogpaddle mixed with breaststroke. Finally she made it and grasped the floating buoy as if it was a lifeline. Slowly, she started to haul the rope up to the buoy.

Sheesh. Sam thought to herself. *She'd go a lot faster if she'd just swim down to the weight rather than pull it up to her!* The women and the cameras on the bank watched as Courtnee slowly went from buoy to buoy. They could see that as Courtnee got to buoys further on in the course it got harder and harder to pull them up to the surface because the weights got heavier

144

and heavier. Finally, after resting a few minutes on one of the last buoys, Courtnee motioned that she was done and wasn't going to attempt to finish the course.

"Five buoys in 23:34," Robert announced. That was the time to beat.

Again, this was another non glamorous part of a reality show. The course had to be reset after each woman went through. That meant that one of the production team had to swim out to each buoy, dive down to get the weight and reattach it. It seemed to take forever to reset. This challenge was going to last all day.

Time passed as each of the other women took their turn in the lake. Some used the same technique as Courtnee, trying to pull the weights up to the buoy, while others tried to swim down to the weight and let it free. The top times with two women left to go were Ashley finishing the course in 26:12 minutes, Kiki finishing the course with a time of 26:30 and Missy making it through six of the seven buoys and weights in 25:42. Finally, it was Sam's turn.

Sam slowly walked down to the bank where Al was waiting. She'd dreaded this part most of all. Al had gotten a good look at the other women, who were mostly all wearing string bikinis of some sort. Lori was the only one who'd been wearing a one piece suit. Sam took off her shorts and then whipped off her T-shirt. It was better to treat this like a Band-Aid, to get it over with quickly rather than slow and painfully. She stood before Al in her one piece black suit. It was one of her practice suits. She tried to get to the pool at least once a week, and this was her most comfortable suit. It was cut high in the legs, but had a keyhole back. She and

Al stood there, looking at each other for a few seconds before Al broke the silence

"You ready?" he asked with a smile. "Do you think you can beat those times?" He sounded hopeful and was looking at her with a pleading look.

Sam *knew* she could, but the question was did she really want to? She knew beating Missy probably wasn't the smartest thing that she could do, it wouldn't help the others like her, but at the same time Sam was a competitive person and she knew she wouldn't be able to not compete and try to win. Besides, she'd really have to make herself look like she couldn't swim in order to pull it off. She tried to ignore the little voice in her head telling her that the real reason she wasn't willing to throw the competition was Al himself. She *wanted* the one-on-one time with him. For once in her life she was going to be selfish. Even if whatever was between her and Al didn't work out in the real world, she'd take this gift that was given to her and enjoy it while she could.

Realizing that Al was waiting for her response, she said cheekily, "I know it, Al, just start thinking about where you want to go on our date!" With that she winked at him and ran toward the water.

Alex laughed and stared after her. Her one piece was definitely more modest than the suits the other women were wearing, but it was no less sexy. In some ways it was sexier. Al watched as the material clung to Sammi's body as she ran. She filled out that suit and then some, and it was sexy as hell. Al thought her ass was perfect in a pair of soaking wet jeans…well, it was nothing compared to that ass in that black suit as she ran toward the water. She was muscular, but he'd

146

noticed that she still had a small bump on her stomach. Somehow that imperfection was real. She was real. She wasn't perfect, but her imperfections made her seem more real. The other women were so model perfect they were almost untouchable. Alex knew if he touched Sammi she'd feel all woman. He was also surprised at her show of almost defiance and playfulness. This was a side he hadn't really seen before and he was eager to see more of it and he hoped she could back up her cockiness with action. He wanted her to be in the top three. He *wanted* the one-on-one time with her.

This was one of the hardest challenges Eddie and the other producers had set up so far. They figured that for the first one-on-one dates they wanted to make the women work a bit harder. Alex and the other women watched as Sam gracefully made her way to the first buoy. She disappeared and Alex was surprised to see her head pop up about a third of the way to the next buoy.

"Not fair!" Missy cried. "Did she even release the weight?"

While Sam was swimming to the next buoy, the producer reassured the women that there were cameras attached to the weights and she'd definitely released it. They all watched as Sam glided through the water toward the other buoys. She made it look effortless. She swam a graceful freestyle stroke. It was obvious to all of the spectators that Sam was comfortable in the water and had possibly swum competitively. Finally, she reached the bank and walked up to the finish line. She'd completed the course in fifteen minutes and four seconds. Sam quickly wrapped a towel around herself and smiled at Al as if to say "told ya so." Alex smiled hugely in return. She'd done it, it felt good to win.

Kathi was the last woman to have her shot at winning the one-on-one date with Al. She'd watched Sammi swimming through the course with growing anger. It wasn't fair that *she* would get one of the coveted spots. There was no way that Al would choose her in the long run. She was short and dumpy. Kathi recalled their conversation in the tent a week or so ago and knew this was her chance. She knew she wasn't going to complete the stupid course. She wasn't that fast or strong of a swimmer. Her idea of "swimming" was to hang out in a hot tub for half an hour. She *could* hold her breath for a long time, however, but she couldn't swim through the water that quickly. She thought fast and came up with a plan. If what Sammi said was true, she'd come out the true winner in this challenge.

Kathi peeled off her clothes and sauntered toward the starting line and Al. She put an extra swing in her step and swayed her butt with her walk. She knew she looked good in her slightly too small red bikini. She put on her best "come hither" smile and walked up to Alex, put her arms around his neck and kissed him. Alex was surprised. Kathi had always been pretty aggressive, but this was different. She was licking along the seam of his lips, seeking entry. There was no way that Alex was going to kiss her in front of the other women. It wasn't right, seeing how he hadn't chosen his winner yet. He refused to open his mouth to Kathi's questing and hopeful tongue and peeled Kathi off of his chest.

"Are you ready?" he asked a bit peevishly.

"I was born ready," Kathi responded. She jogged off toward the water.

They all watched as Kathi reached the first buoy. Like Courtnee, she pulled the rope up rather than swimming down to it. When Kathi reached the second buoy she swam down to the weight. It was quite some time before she resurfaced next to the buoy. She went down again. Obviously she wasn't able to unhook the weight on the first try. Finally, she came up again and swam for the third buoy. She dove down again to untie the rope. Everyone waited for her to come up again. And they waited, and waited some more. Finally, when everyone started to get nervous they saw Kathi's head break the surface. It looked like she was having some difficulties, though. She bobbed up, then went under again. She came up again and then went under again.

Sam started for the lake, but since Al was already there he was faster. He tore off his shirt and started swimming toward the place where they'd last seen Kathi. Everyone was holding their breaths. They saw Al dive down into the water and after what seemed like hours, but in reality was no more than a minute, they saw Al come up with Kathi in a classic lifesaving hold. He had a hold of her around her chest and was swimming the side stroke to shore. Sam could hear Kathi coughing, so she knew she was going to be okay. Coughing meant that she was breathing. The adrenaline was flowing through Sam's and she finally had to sink to the ground. She'd been ready to go out there and find Kathi herself. She didn't like her, but she wasn't going to let her drown!

Alex's heart was beating double time as he swam back toward the shore. For a minute he didn't think he was going to be able to find Kathi. He'd never been so scared. He was glad to hear that she was breathing, but he knew she was going to have to be looked at by a doctor. She'd been under the water for a long time. As Alex neared the shore, he turned Kathi around and held her in his arms. He carried her to shore. Kathi's arms were around his neck and she was still coughing sporadically. He looked at Eddie who by now was also standing lakeside.

"Get a car," Alex said gruffly to Eddie.

Alex gently put Kathi down on the ground near the lake. She curled to her side and continued to cough. Alex rubbed her back and told her to hang on, that they'd be getting her help soon. The other women stood back a bit and watched as Kathi coughed and tried to catch her breath.

She turned toward Al and said hesitantly, "Will you stay with me?" Al nodded and grasped her hand in his.

The producer finally came screaming up with the car, sand spewing everywhere as the car skidded to a halt near the duo. Alex carefully lifted Kathi in his arms again and started for the car that would take them to the hospital to have her checked out. Kathi snuggled into his arms and laid her head on his broad chest.

If Sam hadn't been looking right at Kathi she'd have missed it. Since Sam was standing right next to Courtnee she saw Kathi subtly wink at Courtnee before closing her eyes and lying against Al again. Sam was confused for a second, she heard Kathi moan a bit and wrap her hand around the back of Al's neck. Sam glanced at Courtnee and saw she had a small smirk on her face.

Sam was furious. Kathi was faking it! Sam recalled their conversation about a week ago and knew that she'd inadvertently given Kathi the idea. Al was a protector. He'd do everything in his power to protect them, simply because they were women. It wouldn't matter if he liked the woman or not, he'd do whatever he could to make sure they weren't hurt, and if they were hurt, to nurture them. After all, that was what he'd done with her. Sam felt sick. She couldn't believe Kathi would stoop so low. But it'd been effective. She was wrapped around Al and on her way to the hospital where he could lavish some more TLC on her. She had found a way to get her one-on-one date with him without having to win the competition.

It was a subdued group that made its way back to the bus. Even Robert didn't seem inclined to put on his show airs and announce the winners of the contest. Everything was on hold until Kathi came back from the hospital. Sam already decided to keep her mouth shut. She knew she didn't belong here and there was nothing she hated more than to know that someone was faking an injury. She'd grown up with it in her water polo career. Her teammates were constantly faking some sort of injury to get out of hard practices. Their shoulder hurt, their knee hurt so they couldn't tread water, they had a migraine...the excuses never ended. Sam supposed that was why she hated to show any type of weakness today and why she was mentally stronger than a lot of people.

She couldn't tell Al, he probably wouldn't believe her anyway. She'd tried to tell a coach once that one of her teammates wasn't really hurt and she got in trouble. The coach yelled at her in front of the entire team and made her swim extra laps. The fact that she'd tried to do the right thing and got in trouble for it had already happened once on this show, with the barn incident, and Sam wasn't going to put herself in that position again. The hell with everyone. She knew, however, that she wasn't going to even try to be nice to Kathi after today. And she'd stay away from Courtnee as well. Those two were in this scam together and she wasn't going to have anything to do with it.

The women were all too keyed up to really do much when they got back to camp. They all waited around to see when Kathi was going to come back. Sam hoped they weren't going to keep her overnight. She wondered how she was going to explain to the hospital staff that she wasn't really sick after all.

Eventually, they saw a car pull up. Al got out with Kathi leaning heavily on his arm.

"Thank you, baby, for helping me. I don't know what I would've done without you here. You saved my life," she said, looking up at him with wide eyes. Sam watched cynically as Al walked Kathi to the tent with the rest of the women following along behind. He helped her into the tent, assisted her in lying down, kissed her on the forehead, and covered her with the blanket.

"Sleep, you'll feel better later, I'm sure." Alex turned to the other women who were now inside the bunkhouse with them. "She needs to sleep, make sure you don't bother her. She had a close call today, but she'll be fine. I'll see you all later." And with that he walked out of the bunkhouse, got back in the car and was driven away.

Sam looked sadly at the car driving away from the

camp. A part of her wished that Al had seen through Kathi's rouse. He hadn't even looked at her as he walked away. Maybe it was a sign that the feelings she had for him were only one sided. Hell, she was sure that was it. There was no way he could think she was attractive, especially compared to the other women. She was disappointed in Al. She'd thought he was different. It was an awful feeling to think that she was wrong. That he was like most of the other men she'd met in her life. Superficial and only concerned with his libido.

Sam sighed and came back to the present when the women gathered around Kathi.

"Are you really okay, Kath?" asked Amy with a furrowed brow.

"Oh, yeah," Kathi responded a bit too cheerfully. "Are you kidding? Being carried and held and cosseted by a hunk of a man all afternoon? I'm great, just great." She smiled and looked at everyone. "Worked out better than if I won the competition. I wanted to win a one-on-one date, but I got one anyway and didn't have to finish the stupid course."

Courtnee stood up and shooed everyone back to their bunks and away from Kathi. "She needs to sleep, you heard Al. I'll stay right here and make sure she's all right, the rest of you just go to bed and you can see her later."

The other women grumbled a bit, but went back to their bunks.

"Okay, give!" Courtnee said to Kathi in a low voice as soon as everyone was away from their sides. "I want to know every detail!"

Kathi and Courtnee talked for over an hour. Kathi

told her new friend all about how concerned Al was, how he wouldn't leave her side, and when she thought she was losing his attention all she had to do was moan a bit and he'd be looking at her with concern all over again. He held her hand just about the entire time. She told Courtnee how Alex had helped her into the hospital gown since all she'd been wearing was her bikini. Kathi told Courtnee all about how she faked the coughing and the pain in her chest when the doctor was examining her. She did have to get an x-ray done to make sure there wasn't any more fluid in her lungs, though. They laughed at that since there'd never been any fluid in there in the first place since she held her breath the entire time she was underwater. They laughed at how Kathi had taken the wind right out of Sammi's sails after her great performance.

"Al didn't even mention the contest or the show the entire time we were together," Kathi gushed. Kathi was pleased with herself. She knew she'd made a great impression on Al and she couldn't wait to see him again and show him she was better, but not *too* much better and that she needed some more TLC.

Chapter Fifteen

"God, what a day," Alex said out loud, even though no one was in his tent listening to him. This had to be one of the scariest days of his life. He'd almost seen another human being, a woman at that, die in front of his eyes. It'd taken everything he had to not break down in front of everyone when he knew Kathi was going to be okay. Kathi was really scared and she was obviously in a lot of pain on the way to the hospital. He'd held her the entire way. While he was scared for her, he was also a man and couldn't help but remember how well she fit into his arms. She was a good looking woman and he couldn't help but think about how they might fit together outside of the show.

Once they got to the hospital he stayed by her side for as much of the examination as he could. The doctor told them she wasn't any worse for wear and that she could return to the show. She seemed to be better on her way back to the camp, almost back to normal, but once they pulled up and saw the other women waiting and watching for them she seemed to get weak again. He couldn't understand it, but was certainly glad that she was on the mend. She'd scared ten years off his life!

Alex gathered a clean set of clothes and headed to the communal bathroom to take a quick shower. He could hear the excitement around the camp. This would make for great television once the show aired. He was under the impression that sometimes he still didn't know what was going on, even though he was able to watch the tapes from camp each night. He really didn't think it was appropriate for Kathi's near death to be made into "must see" TV, but he knew that what he thought didn't matter to Eddie. He'd do what he needed to do to make his show successful.

Later that night when he was relaxing in his tent he heard a soft "Alex?" come from outside his door. It was Kina. He remembered she was the camera operator that had shared her concerns about Sammi after the snake incident. She slid into his open tent after Alex invited her in and handed him a tape.

"I've already watched the day's tapes," he told her, shuddering as he remembered watching Kathi in the water and his rescue from earlier.

"This is the tape that Eddie didn't want you to see," she told him solemnly. "When you are done watching it, put it out behind your tent and I'll grab it and put it back so he doesn't notice that it's gone." And with that Kina slipped out the door.

Alex wondered what was on the tape and why he hadn't been allowed to see it earlier. What was Eddie trying to keep from him? He got pissed just thinking about it. He'd *known* all along that Eddie was sneaky, but he'd hoped he was being honest with him. Alex glanced at the tape in his hand and sincerely hoped it wasn't of the women getting dressed or something just as offensive. He just didn't feel right watching that, although the women didn't seem to care that a camera was watching them inside their bunkhouse.

He put the tape in the player and watched the scene from earlier that night as he helped Kathi to her bed. This was the tape from inside the bunkhouse at the women's camp. Alex watched as he walked out the door and Courtnee shooed everyone away from Kathi and back to their own bunks.

Alex couldn't believe what he saw on the tape. He knew that the contestants on shows like this could be one person in public and another person when interacting with the other contestants, but he never saw this coming. This was low. This was beyond low. Alex rewound the tape three times to watch Kathi and Courtnee talk about Kathi's "accident." He'd never been so furious in all of his life. She'd done it on purpose! She wasn't drowning, she'd only pretended to be in trouble in the water and had used him. If he was back in his world he would've destroyed her, but he wasn't. He was here in the Outback on a ridiculous dating show with ridiculous women who thought they could manipulate him. He felt ashamed at how he'd felt earlier in the day with Kathi in his arms. He'd been holding a barracuda.

At first he wanted to storm into Eddie's tent and quit. He was disillusioned and couldn't believe that anyone could stoop as low as Kathi had today. He thought about all the other times he was with the women and wondered how else he'd been manipulated by either the women or by Eddie. He wanted to lump all the women in the same category as Kathy and Courtnee, but something wouldn't let him. He thought about Lori and Amy and Sammi. He felt relatively sure that they, at least, were one hundred percent honest with him. He thought about it a long time. He thought about what his next move should be. If Kathi wanted to make herself seem as if she was a completely different kind of person, he'd play it her way…for now.

Alex put the tape outside where he and Kina

arranged, and lay back down on his bed. There had to be a reason why Eddie didn't want him to see the tape. He wondered again what else he hadn't seen. While the production team might have made him think he was one of "them" it was obvious now that they were using him as much as they were using the girls. It was all about the ratings, and they didn't care who got hurt in the process. He was done playing by their rules. He'd tried, but they'd upped the ante. He'd play their game, but he had a few aces up his sleeve as well.

Chapter Sixteen

Sam was still pissed the next day. Since she'd placed first in the competition her time with Al would be the last one-on-one date and it wouldn't be until the next day. Kiki was going on her date this morning and Ashley would be going on her own that afternoon. It was a good day to relax, but that was something Sam was finding hard to do. She remembered Kathi's performance that morning about how she should have the first shot at the shower since she was still weak. Whatever.

Sam and the rest of the women watched as a giant hot-air balloon slowly appeared to the west of the camp. Holy Crap! Kiki's transportation had arrived. The balloon gracefully landed and Al climbed out. He first walked over to Kathi to see if she was feeling better. She told him yes, but that she was still weak.

Alex responded, "Make sure you get some rest today then," and grasped her hand in his, kissing the back of it.

Then he turned around and walked up to Kiki and took her by the hand. They walked back toward the huge balloon and Alex assisted Kiki into getting into the basket of the balloon. Everyone watched the balloon rise up into the air until it couldn't be seen anymore.

Kathi immediately huddled with Courtnee to compare notes about Al's attention to her and what it meant. Sam was disgusted. She knew she'd told herself she wasn't going to walk around by herself anymore, but damn it, she needed that time alone. Nothing was really going on at camp so there was only one camera around to film. Sam figured it was because most of cameras were scheduled to film the dates, which was definitely more interesting than the rest of them just sitting around. Sam knew she could sneak away without being followed, either by the other contestants or a camera operator.

Sam climbed up the rise to her spot she'd spent quite a bit of time at, and found a comfortable spot where she sat and tried to relax. She thought about the last few days and the other women. She thought about Al, what she liked and didn't like about him. It was ironic that she'd be going on a one-on-one date with him because she was probably the only woman who really didn't care that much about "winning" him. Sam knew relationships formed by these reality dating shows usually didn't end up working in the end. There were a few—maybe two—that had, but those were few and far between.

She did like Al, he seemed to be a gentleman and he was polite to all of them. She was also very attracted to him. How could anyone not find him attractive? But how well did she really *know* him? How well did any of them know him? What was his favorite color? Did he have any siblings? Were his parents still alive? What kind of music did he listen to? There were about a million other things she wanted to know about him. If this was a normal courtship she'd probably already know some of the answers. Some of the contestants wanted to "win" so they could become famous and perhaps have an active career launched. Others wanted to win because Al was rich.

All Sam had ever wanted out of her life was to be content. She got lonely, but she wasn't about to marry someone for the sake of marrying them. Her life was just fine. She was employed, had a place to live, and was happy with her life. There were times on the weekends or when she wasn't that busy that she wished she had someone to talk to and share her thoughts with other than her three dogs, but not enough to tie herself to anyone just for the sake of being married.

Sam heard a commotion back at the camp. She sat up and realized she'd fallen asleep. She strolled down to the camp in time to see Ashley and Al getting into a Hummer. Obviously, Al and Kiki made it back from their date.

Al helped Ashley into the passenger seat and leaned over her to buckle her seatbelt. It was a very gentlemanly thing to do. Sam's belly tightened. Everything she'd told herself while sitting on the rise felt like a lie watching Al take care of Ashley. She never thought she was the type of woman who would enjoy that type of pampering, but Al was quickly changing her mind. Sam could practically see the other women sighing at Al's actions as well. As they drove off, the other women gathered around Kiki to hear all about her date.

Sam wasn't really interested, but figured it might be enlightening to listen. She might get a better insight into Al's personality and she might learn more about him. Kiki talked about how they were in the balloon for a while and how Al was so protective when she got scared. He held her hand while they landed to help calm her down. They landed at a site that overlooked a valley. There was a lunch all set up for them. She exclaimed about how much of a gentleman Al was and how romantic the entire thing was.

In Sam's eyes it sounded a bit contrived, but she wasn't there, so she had to take Kiki's word for it. That was a problem. Who knew what the truth was and what was embellished by Kiki showing off. After they ate, Kiki explained, they went and sat under a tree. Al held her to him as they talked about what they wanted out of life and what they wanted out of this reality show experience. Kiki said that the mood was just getting right when they had to leave. She didn't get to kiss him, except on the cheek, but she was damn sure not going to let the opportunity pass her by again.

Sam sighed. It sounded wonderful all right, but she now knew not to trust anyone and what they said. Again, who knew what really happened on the date. The rest of the day passed slowly. The women were anxious to hear back from Ashley and see what she did on their date. They were bored with themselves and really wanted something to do. Even Courtnee seemed to be getting irritated with Kathi after spending large amounts of time with her.

Evening fell and still Ashley and Al weren't back. A bonfire was lit around the fire ring and most of the women sat outside and watched the flames.

Suddenly, they heard Ashley's voice, "What a beautiful night!" They all turned around to see her walking back into camp and into the fire circle. Everyone started talking at once. Where was Al? How was the date? What did they do?

Ashley held up her hand. "Is everyone here? I only want to tell it once."

Finally, once they were all settled around the fire Ashley talked about her day. They'd driven to a small air strip where they'd then gotten on a small airplane. Al had been the pilot—which got lots of sighs since no one knew he was a pilot too—and after about twenty minutes they landed on a dusty airstrip. At first it didn't look like there was anything around, but Al led Ashley toward a wooded stand of trees, and there was a picnic set up for them. They sat and talked and ate. Afterward Al wanted to go for a walk, but Ashley told him she'd rather sit and talk some more. Ashley explained how they talked into the evening and it wasn't until it was getting dark that they realized what time it was and that he had to get her back.

"We stood up and Al took me into his arms. He looked into my eyes, said my name and gave me the sweetest kiss you can imagine." She enthused.

Most of the women thought that was the most romantic thing they'd ever heard, but Sam could also see that most of them were jealous as hell and resolved to do whatever they could in the future challenges to be the one in Al's arms. She just shook her head. It sounded good, but again, how much was truth and how much was embellishment?

Missy suddenly turned to Sam and said, "So what do you think you'll be doing tomorrow?"

"I have no idea," Sam responded slowly. "But in keeping with the theme of the last two dates, I'm sure it'll be something extravagant."

* * *

The next morning Sam made sure she was the first

163

one out of bed so she could use the shower first and be ready to meet Al. She wouldn't put it past some of the girls, especially Kathi, to try to sabotage her "getting ready" time. She was actually looking forward to the date. For one thing it would get her out of the camp and away from Kathi and Courtnee, for another she really did want to get to know Al better. She wasn't sure if she could really trust him, but she'd try to give him the benefit of the doubt.

When Al pulled up in a dirty jeep about twenty minutes after she'd gotten out of the shower, Sam was doubly glad that she'd awakened early that day. Half of the women weren't even out of bed yet. Sam went over to meet him.

"Good morning," Alex said softly.

"Good morning to yourself," Sam replied.

"You ready to go?" Alex asked with a gleam in his eye.

"Sure, do I need to bring anything special?" Sam inquired.

"Just yourself," Alex told her as he took her hand and led her to the jeep.

"Not quite the exit that you had yesterday, huh?" Sam asked with a smile, not able to hold back the question.

Alex laughed and told her, "I figured this would be more your speed…was I right?"

Sam looked at him and told him honestly with some surprise, "You pegged me right. I think I would've been scared to be in the balloon, and the Humvee was a bit over the top. But I like this jeep, let's hope it won't die on us as we're out in the middle of the Outback." They both laughed as Al helped her

into her seat. Just as he did with Ashley, he leaned over
her and snapper her seatbelt into place. It seemed to
Sammi that he stood over her for just a beat longer
than was necessary to snap the belt into place, but
before she could ask him if anything was wrong he
stood up and walked around the jeep.

Alex climbed in the driver's seat, pulled the
seatbelt across his strong chest, clipped it in and started
up the jeep. "Naw, Betty wouldn't let me down, not
with the precious cargo she's carrying today."

Sam rolled her eyes at Al. "Give me a break, not
even five minutes into this date and you are already
talking crap!"

They both laughed as Alex drove out of the camp.
"I'd never talk crap to you Sammi," he said seriously.
"Anything I tell you is one hundred percent the truth."

Sam looked around and suddenly asked, "Where's
the camera?"

"I have no idea," Alex answered, "but I'm not
going to look a gift horse in the mouth."

"Should we go back and see if we have to pick
someone up?" Sammi asked seriously. She didn't want
to get in trouble for ditching the camera operator. It
seemed like that would be an offense that could get her
kicked off the show in a heartbeat.

Alex *had* wondered why he hadn't seen a camera,
but he figured maybe it was going to be at their
destination and told Sammi that very thing.

Sammi shrugged and asked Al as they bumped
along the road, "So where are we going?"

"I thought about giving you a choice on what you
wanted to do today," Alex told her, "but then I thought
I'd make it a surprise for you. How come you never

165

told me you could swim?" Alex asked her expectantly out of the blue.

Sam laughed. "You never asked," she told him with a smile.

Alex smiled back at her. She had a point. He didn't really have to ask much about the other women because they generally told him everything they could about themselves, whether he wanted to know it or not. He hadn't been alone with Sammi much since the show started. He found himself for the hundredth time wanting to know about her, her likes and dislikes. He knew a little about her personality from watching the tapes, and he knew that she was different from the other women, but he remembered how the producers had tricked him, and wondered if there were more tricks up their sleeves.

"What do you think of the show so far?" he asked Sammi.

Sam thought for a minute. "It's a lot what I thought it would be, but at the same time not."

"Can you explain?" Alex responded, honestly wanting to know how she felt about the show, and indirectly about him.

Sam paused to gather her thoughts before answering. "I mean, I knew that these "reality" shows weren't really "reality," and there was a lot that the audience didn't see. I also thought since this was a "dating" show things would get pretty intense, but I guess I didn't expect the level of intensity from both the producers and the other contestants." Sam looked at Alex as he drove. "I mean, I like you, I think you're a great guy, but everyone around here is acting like you are the last man on the planet and if they don't

166

"win" then they'll end up single for the rest of their lives…I don't get that." Sam ended softly.

Alex was surprised at her insight. "I know what you mean," he told her. "I thought I'd come on the show, meet some great women, get to know them and BAM, be struck head over heels by cupid's arrow."

"Hasn't happened, huh?" Sam asked with a grin.

"I'm getting there," Alex told her mysteriously with a lift of his eyebrow. Suddenly, he got solemn again. "I know what you mean, though. It's that disillusionment. I knew there'd be some women on the show who were just doing it for the exposure and, of course, my money. I see that all the time back home, but with all the twists and turns in this show it's hard to really know what everyone wants and what they're really thinking."

Sam nodded as Alex continued, "And I'm scared to death that I'll really like someone, and then find out that their whole personality is a lie. That everything they've said to me was a carefully crafted effort to "catch" me."

Sam shifted uneasily, thinking about Kathi and her schemes.

Suddenly, Alex pulled the jeep off to the side of the road and turned to Sam. He put his hand on the back of her chair and played with her hair unconsciously. Sam shivered. It felt so good to have him touching her, even if it was only her hair. She felt it down to her bones and shivered with the sensuality of his actions. She forced herself to pay attention to him as he started speaking.

"Tell me what you think of the other women," he said earnestly. He wanted to know what she thought, but he also wanted to know what she knew about Kathi. When he'd asked Ashley and Kiki about what they thought about the other contestants, they were all too happy to tell him all sorts of negative things about everyone. He felt a disappointed that they were so eager to trash talk everyone else.

Sam looked at him with indecision. She'd never been the type of person to tell tales about other people, but she also really liked Al and didn't want him to make any decisions that he would regret when the show was over.

She decided to tell the truth as much as she could, "I like Amy, Ashley, and Lori. They are pretty friendly and seem to like you a lot. I think you should choose one of them," she told him with as much enthusiasm as she could muster.

"Not you?" Alex asked with a smile.

Sam laughed a little sadly. "We both know I'm not going to make it to the finals," she told him, holding up her hand to forestall his comment. "Look at me, I don't know how I even made it onto the show, but I'm definitely different from the other women. Personally, I think it was a mistake. I think somehow the producers messed up when they picked me. Television is about looking good, and while I certainly don't think that I'm hideous, I can't hold a candle to the other women here. I don't know who's deciding who stays and who goes when there aren't competitions, but I bet the producers want the "pretty" people to end up last."

Alex looked at her in shock. "They wouldn't do that. Look at yourself. Seriously. You're beautiful." At her snort he continued a bit sternly. "Honestly, I wouldn't lie to you. Not all men want a woman who is skin and bones. While you have a soft glow about you, you also have a backbone of steel. I know I could be with you, in bed, and you wouldn't break," Alex said with a smile. He'd had the same suspicions lately about Eddie and the other producers and thought they were manipulating things a bit as well.

Sam blushed a fiery red at Al's comment about them in bed. She'd also thought about it, but wasn't about to admit it to him. "Well, anyway, thank you for that, but I know my appeal, and if we were in the "real" world, I know a man like you would never look twice at me."

"And what kind of man am I?" Alex asked her, irritation sounding in his voice, knowing she was probably right about if he met her back home in Austin, in his normal environment, he might not have asked her out.

"Gorgeous and successful, the kind of man who could have any woman he wanted," Sam told him honestly.

They sat there looking at each other for a long moment.

"A couple of weeks ago I was cursing myself for agreeing to be on this show," he told her earnestly, "but now, I'm thanking my lucky stars. Do you believe in fate, Sammi?" he asked.

"No," Sam said without pause. "I think we're lucky to meet someone that we can love and get along with, but I don't necessarily believe that there is only one person out there for each of us."

Alex knew that the conversation was getting pretty intense and was determined to lighten it up a bit.

"Okay, you told me who I *should* pick, so why not

the others? What about Kathi or Missy? They seem very nice." Alex watched her reaction carefully. He knew what kind of person Kathi was, and honestly wasn't sure about the others. He wanted to know what Sammi thought. If he was completely honest with himself it was also a bit of a test.

"You're going to have to make up your own mind about them," Sam told him firmly. "I'm not going to get in the middle of a fight over you. And if they hear I was talking about you that's what will happen." She tried to smile at him. She didn't want to lie to him, but she didn't want to tell him her opinions either. They were *her* opinions after all. "Are we going to get on with this mystery date or what?" she asked playfully, changing the subject, deciding that the conversation had gotten way too serious for a first date.

"Okay, okay, I'll let the subject drop. But I only asked you because I value your opinion, you know," Alex told her. He smiled and let the subject drop. "Let our date begin."

* * *

They drove for a while and finally arrived at a small town. It was more civilization than Sam had seen in a while now. She didn't say anything to Al, figuring he'd tell her what was up in his own time. They pulled into a parking lot that was across the street from a small amusement park. It looked like one of the same traveling fairs that occasionally set up back home. Sam looked at Alex in confusion.

"Is this okay?" Alex asked with a bit of trepidation. "You seemed like the kind of person who would enjoy having some fun."

Sam beamed and resisted clapping her hands and jumping up and down in her seat like a lunatic. "It's perfect. I'm not sure I'd know what to do with myself if we did the "lunch by the river" thing!"

Alex smiled back and thought she was the cutest thing he'd ever seen. He loved that she wasn't afraid to show her excitement about their day. As they walked toward the entrance to the carnival he grabbed her hand. He looked at Sammi with his eyebrow raised as if to ask if it was okay. Sam smiled, squeezed his hand reassuringly and they continued on.

They spent the better part of the morning on all of the rides, some more than once. They hadn't noticed any cameras around, which they both still thought was odd, but they were having so much fun, they didn't even care. Alex kept a hold of Sam's hand as much as he could. When they were on the one roller coaster she held it tight. When they went on the "zipper" Sam buried her head in his shoulder. She'd always hated going upside down on rides, but Alex had dared her to ride it with him and of course she never turned down a dare! All in all it was a great morning. They laughed, a lot, and there was no more serious talk about the show or the other women.

Finally, they'd had enough of the park and decided to go to lunch.

"Where would you like to go?" Alex asked Sammi as they headed back toward the jeep.

"Anywhere is good. I don't really like seafood, but I can usually find something to eat in a seafood restaurant if you really want to go to one," she told him.

"We could get something to go and eat it in a nearby park that I saw." He suggested, rubbing his thumb over the top of her hand as they were talking.

"Okay, you pick," Sam told him, distracted by his nearness and by the goose bumps that spread over her arms at his touch.

Sam laughed when she saw his pick of restaurant. It was a popular fast-food burger place they had back in the States.

"This okay?" Alex asked nervously, knowing that she might not want to eat the greasy food.

"Oh my God! It's perfect!" Sam laughed. "I've been craving their French fries!"

They ordered their lunch and set out for the park. Alex parked the jeep and held up his hand for her to wait as she was about to get it. He ran around the front of the jeep and opened the door for her. He held out his hand in a gallant gesture and helped her to the ground. They found an empty table in the middle of the park under a tree that was throwing a lot of shade. Sam sat down and was surprised when Al sat next to her rather than on the other side of the table. They ate their lunch and laughed and joked with each other. Sam asked most of the questions she'd been thinking about yesterday. She honestly felt as if she knew him a lot better after they'd eaten and talked. It was a good feeling. After they were finished Alex swung one leg over the bench seat and encouraged Sammi to do the same.

"What are you doing?" she asked him.

"Shhhh, just swing your leg over and put your back to me." Alex soothed her, holding on to her hips and turning her as he spoke.

Sam did as he asked and he pulled her back to rest against his chest.

They sat there for a while, just enjoying the feeling of being close to another human being and watching the other people in the park. Alex finally broke the silence.

"I'd like to think that if we'd met somewhere before this show, that I would've been interested," he said quietly with his breath tickling Sam's ear. "I know in the past that I've been somewhat of a ladies man, but this show, and you, have taught me what I really want."

"And what is it you really want?" Sam asked, turning her head around to look at him.

"I want someone I can laugh with. I want a woman who I can sit on a park bench and not speak, but still be comfortable with. I want a woman who wants me for who I am, not for what I can give her. I want a woman who can be my friend as well as my lover. I want a woman who will stand in the rain with me just because it's there and not worry about her makeup or her hair. I want a woman who's strong, but who can still lean on me. I want to look forward to going home because I know that she's there. I want a woman I can take care of. Who will let me pamper her just because I want to."

Alex took a deep breath and looked down at Sammi. "I want a companion. I want someone to call my own and a woman who can call me hers."

Alex saw a tear fall from Sammi's eye. He reached up with his finger to brush it away. "I want this," he said softly and dipped his head to her lips. Alex's hand went to the back of Sam's neck and tightened, drawing her to him. His lips moved on hers. Sam let out a short moan.

Alex ran his tongue along the seam of her lips, tracing the opening as if asking permission. When he was about to pull away Sam's tongue came out to meet his. Alex took the moment and plunged inside. Since Sam was bent at an odd angle, with her back still to his front, her hand snaked up and grabbed the back of Alex's neck as if to anchor him to her. Alex's other arm came around her waist and pulled her closer. Sam could feel his hard length in the small of her back.

Sam could barely think. God. It was as if her brain had turned to mush. Had she ever been this turned on with her other boyfriends? Had a kiss ever made her want to throw all caution to the winds and give in? His tongue ran over her teeth and dueled with her tongue. He thrust his tongue in and out of her mouth as if telling her how he'd take her if they were in bed together. Finally, Alex eased away, panting. He rested his cheek alongside her head and she turned to face forward again.

"I probably should apologize for that, but I won't," he told her in a hoarse voice. Sam could feel his heart beating against her body as well as his shaft hard against her back. "I don't know what it is between us, but I've never felt like this." Alex took her earlobe between his teeth and bit down softly.

Sam shivered. Her ears and neck had always been sensitive. It was hard to think with his arm across her body, his hand resting at her hip and his breath gliding over her neck.

"I know, I think I feel the same way," she answered breathlessly, hardly knowing what she was saying.

"You think?" Alex whispered in her ear.

"I don't know what to make of this," Sam answered honestly, determined to get this out. "I mean, I heard all about your other dates and how romantic they were. Essentially you're dating nine women at the same time. It's just hard for me to believe that you aren't saying these things to the others as well."

Alex disentangled himself from her, stood up and squatted down next to the bench, looking up at Sam. He wrapped one hand behind her neck gently and palmed her cheek with the other hand. He looked into her eyes and willed her to believe him as he answered her concerns.

"I swear, Sammi, the other dates I've been on were completely innocent compared to what I'm feeling here. I know we don't know what'll happen and how this game will turn out, but I want you to know that I'm being completely honest with you. I don't want to lie to you. I hope you feel the same about me."

Sam looked at Al. She was scared, she hadn't lied to him. He was everything she'd ever want in a man. She wanted all the same things that he did. When he was talking earlier about what he wanted in a woman, she could imagine herself doing all those things with him, being that woman, and it scared her to death. What did she really know about him? They were practically strangers. Was this just a result of being isolated in the Outback and him being the only available guy around? It wasn't like they could feel their way and take things slowly. She was in a competition. She could lose tomorrow. Her heart hurt when she thought about that. But Sam was also practical. She knew you couldn't have everything you wanted in life and this might not turn out the way she wanted it to. Then there was the honesty that Al was pleading with her to give him. She knew she should tell him about Kathi and the stunt she'd pulled at the lake, but it wasn't her place, it really wasn't. She wouldn't stoop to Kathi's level to win. She'd just have to make sure Al wanted *her* around, and not the other women.

"I do feel the same and I'll do my best to be honest with you. I don't know if this is just our circumstances or if it would be like this between us back in the States, but rest assured that it's not one sided," she told him.

Alex beamed. "Awesome!" he said softly, leaning forward at the same time pulling her head toward him. He took her mouth again, not waiting for her to reciprocate, but plunging inside with enthusiasm. They finally pulled apart when a group of boys walking by yelled out "Get a room!"

Sam blushed and noticed that her hands were holding on to his arms with her fingernails digging in. Alex leaned his forehead against hers and said, "Unfortunately, I think we have to head back, it's getting late. At the crestfallen look on her face, he said in a softer voice, "I know, I don't want to go either, but think about it this way, the faster we get back, the faster this game will be over!"

So they packed up their trash and headed back to the jeep hand in hand. All too soon they were nearing the camp. Sam sighed.

"What was that sigh for?" Alex asked, looking at

her with concern.

"It's just hitting me that it's really over," Sam said, smiling at Al. "I'm just preparing myself for the third degree."

"What are you going to tell them?" Alex asked.

"The truth." Sam paused until Al looked at her with a furrow between his brows. "That we spent the day at a carnival, ate lunch, then came back. What happens between us is between us." She finished.

Alex smiled at her. "God, thank you for that. Trust me to keep our time together private as well."

Sam smiled at him. As they pulled up into the camp the other women were walking toward the jeep to meet them. She reluctantly let go of Al's hand and felt his thumb rub over the back of her one last time before he let go. Sam knew the women weren't coming over to see her, they just wanted another chance to talk to Al. Alex helped her out of the jeep and leaned down to place a chaste kiss on her cheek while giving her a short squeeze on her waist. Sam blushed a bit.

Alex smiled at her and said, "Until next time." He nodded hello to the other women in general, got back in the jeep and drove away. As soon as the jeep was gone the others wanted to know what happened on their date. Sam told them only enough to appease their curiosity and escaped to the bunkhouse to dream about Al.

Susan Stoker

Chapter Seventeen

The "vote out" was supposed to be the same day as Sam's date, but since they got back later than they were supposed to Eddie decided the light wasn't good and they'd have to wait until the next day. When Alex got back to his camp he sought Eddie out.

"I've decided who I want to go next," he told him without preamble. "After careful consideration I don't think that Kathi and I have much in common."

The producer looked surprised.

"Sorry, we need to keep her around for a bit longer," the producer told him without remorse.

"What?!? Why?" asked Alex, although he had a feeling he knew why.

"She was just hurt the other day, it makes for great TV. Viewers are going to want to see how she's doing and how she's healing. And since you played Sir Galahad we're going to play that up a bit," the producer answered.

Alex was pissed. He knew it. He *knew* he was being played. He couldn't tell Eddie that he knew Kathi faked her accident. He wasn't supposed to have seen the tape in the first place. On the other hand he knew he'd be hard pressed to act civil around her.

The producer continued, "I think it's time that Sammi goes home."

"No way!" Alex responded immediately with heat. "I thought I was the one who decided who'd stay and who'd go!"

"Look," Eddie reasoned, "We're here to make

money. Sammi doesn't fit in. We honestly don't even know how she got on the show. We think there was a mix up between her and another woman named Sammi. Somehow someone invited the wrong woman, and by the time we realized it, she'd already signed the contract so we couldn't make her leave. We let her stay on for a while because she was entertaining, but it's time that she goes. America doesn't want to watch overweight women on TV. That's their everyday reality. We need to give them the glamorous side of people, make them want to tune in every week to see which babe you'll end up with."

Alex was so furious he was shaking. Sammi had been right all along.

"First of all she isn't "overweight. Second of all am I or am I not choosing the final contestants?"

"Well," Eddie hedged, "you have a say...to a point. If we don't think you're making the right choice, we'll make it for you. It's not like you have to stay with this woman forever, just until the end of the show and the publicity tours on the talk shows after its aired. We tout this show as a man finding his soul mate. Everyone knows that probably won't happen, so we just want to have good TV along the way. And if that means us telling you who'll stay and who'll go, then so-be-it."

Between clenched teeth, Alex asked, "Who will the final two contestants be then?"

"We're not sure, but we have a general idea, and Sammi sure isn't one of them," the producer answered and pretend gagged, not realizing how on the edge Alex was.

Alex was beyond pissed. Eddie was a horrible

person. He didn't care who he hurt as he clawed his way upward. If there was a way to get off the show he'd do it, but he knew he'd signed an iron clad contract, and there was no way they'd let him go now with the show half way over.

"At least let her stay through one more round," Alex practically begged. He couldn't imagine what she'd think if after their date and that kiss, she left now. He especially didn't want her to think that *he* voted her off. Besides all that, he desperately wanted her to stay. He *liked* her. She was perhaps the only woman on the show that he *did* like.

The producer looked at Alex for a long time and finally bit out, "Fine. We'll get rid of Cindee tomorrow."

"Fine," parroted Alex. He gave Eddie a hard look and said, "you'd better not be lying to me."

"Cindee will be the one who goes tomorrow," Eddie promised. Alex knew that he couldn't trust him, but had no choice. He finally nodded and walked away.

Shit. He thought as he walked back to his tent. That hadn't gone well. He knew that these reality shows probably weren't true "reality," but this was ridiculous. He didn't want to see Sammi go, and he certainly didn't want to have to pretend to actually like Kathi or some of the others that were left. He had to talk to Sammi. He knew he wasn't supposed to, but she already had some idea that she was going to be kicked off soon. He just wanted her to know it wasn't him who wanted her gone.

* * *

The next morning Alex met Robert and the women at their camp for the "vote off." The nine women looked nervous, but composed as usual. Alex had purposely gotten to the camp right before the cameras would start rolling so he wouldn't have to talk to any of them. He just wasn't up to pretending he was glad to see them, when all he wanted to do was talk to Sammi alone and let her know what was going on. The only drawback of arriving late was that he couldn't talk to Sammi at all before the stupid ceremony. He consoled himself with the fact that he'd talk to her after the ceremony and let her know what Eddie had said about the mix up in the invitation to the show. He didn't want to hurt her feelings, but she had to know. He'd promised to be honest with her.

As the ceremony began, Robert went into a speech about how it had been an interesting couple of days and he recounted the adventures at the lake and the three one-on-one dates. He asked the women to go around and tell Alex why they felt they should get to stay on the show. He asked a few pointed questions to some of the women about how they were feeling about Al and the other women. The women were on their best behavior, very aware of the television cameras and kept their answers pretty civil. Finally, Robert got to the point.

"The eighth person who will be leaving Australia will be…Cindee." Cindee gasped and immediately started crying.

It was a bit awkward around the circle as Cindee stood in place and cried but no one told her which way to walk away to leave the show.

Finally Robert said, "Cindee, unfortunately you have to leave Australia, and Al, but there is a twist today." He paused dramatically. The women looked at him expectantly. Alex looked at him with trepidation. He had a bad feeling about this.

"Throughout the show the women who've gone home have left either because they were unlucky enough to have their name chosen at random, or they lost a challenge. Today, Cindee, you get to change the game." Cindee and the others just stared at Robert perplexed. Alex felt his teeth clench. He knew he wasn't going to like how Cindee would get to change the game. Damn Eddie.

"I wouldn't call today your lucky day, since you're going home, but you aren't the only unlucky woman here today. Someone else will also be leaving." Everyone gasped.

"Cindee, you get to choose one of the remaining women that will be leaving today as well."

Alex covered his indignation with a cough. He thought back to his conversation with Eddie the night before. He hadn't said that Cindee would be the *only* woman going home. He only promised that she'd be going home. Alex looked across the distance at Sammi in despair and found that she was looking at him. She had a grim look on her face, almost resigned. It was as if she knew what the outcome of today would be. They both ultimately knew who Cindee would choose to leave with her. He wanted to mouth 'I'm sorry' to Sammi, but was afraid the cameras would pick it up. He tried to convey his angst to her from afar. He held her eyes until she broke their eye contact and looked at the ground.

183

Cindee took a deep breath. Her tear ravaged face took in the women standing around, all staring at her, wondering who her choice would be.

"Wow," Cindee started rather dramatically, "I never expected this. This is going to be a tough decision. I've had a great time with everyone, and I can't imagine being the one to make someone have to leave." She paused to let her insincere speech sink in. Cindee knew she was in the spotlight and it was her time to shine. She continued on with her speech. Rambling on about the good times she'd had while on the show and how much she was going to miss everyone. She talked about how she wasn't sure how she was going to choose someone and how it wasn't fair, but someone had to go.

Sam looked up at Al again. She wondered why he looked so mad. She somehow knew this was going to be her last day at the camp and on the show. She knew she didn't fit in and there certainly wasn't any love lost between her and Cindee. After her date yesterday she'd sure miss Al, she honestly thought that maybe the two of them could've possibly made it. For a brief moment the night before she dreamed about winning the show and having Al choose *her* at the end. But she'd never find out now. She caught Al looking at her again. She gave him a sad smile and shook her head slightly.

"I suppose since I have to choose someone, it would have to be…Sammi," Cindee finally said. Sam walked forward to where Robert and Cindee were standing. Cindee had a smug look on her face.

"Sammi, Cindee has made her choice," Robert droned, "Please say your goodbyes and Al will walk you to the car."

Cindee and the other women spent a bit of time crying and saying goodbye. Sam heard some of them thanking Cindee, not very quietly. She shrugged. Sam didn't bother going over to the other women. She knew what they thought of her and the thought of them pretending they were sad she was leaving was just too much. She walked toward Al.

Alex held his hand out toward Sammi as she walked toward him. She put her hand in his. They walked to the car.

"This wasn't my decision," he started desperately, knowing their time together was short, but stopped when Sammi put her fingers on his lips.

"I know, it was inevitable." Sam looked at Al, she had to say it. She leaned toward him and hugged him. At the same time she put her lips at his ear and said, "If you're given the choice to pick someone you need to choose either Lori or Amy."

Alex looked at her earnest face. "Can you tell me why?" he asked softly.

"I can't, I wish I could, but I can't. Just please trust me," Sam practically begged him.

Alex squeezed Sammi desperately. He turned his head so now his mouth was by her ear and told her, "I trust you. God, I trust you. This isn't over, Sammi. I don't think I can let you go. You *will* hear from me again." He nipped her earlobe lightly and stepped backward. He leaned forward, gave her a hard kiss on the lips, and turned back toward the other women without another word.

Sam climbed into the waiting car. She refused to look back as the car drove off. A lone tear tracked down her face. It wasn't fair, but she expected it, she just didn't know how much it would hurt. She wasn't TV material and she knew it. She wasn't skinny enough and her boobs weren't big enough. Sam recalled Alex's last words. She wasn't sure what he meant, but she knew it was going to be a long time between now and when the show aired.

The car dropped Sam off at a small airstrip. She was taken back to the city and checked into a hotel. The phone was removed from the room so she couldn't call anyone back home and was told she'd have to stay at the hotel until the end of the show. There weren't any other contestants staying at the hotel so they wouldn't be able to "trade" stories from the show. Sam was given a coupon book for several local tours that she could take to fill up her time until the show ended. Sam sighed. All she wanted to do was go home to her job, her friends and her dogs. The show had taken a lot out of her. She knew she and Al had pretty good chemistry, but it looked like it wasn't meant to be. She hoped he took her advice about who to choose if he could. Amy and Lori really were the littlest of all the evils. They weren't perfect, but they were much nicer than the other women. Sam knew she'd get practically no more communication from the producers about the show or what was going on. She'd have to watch like the rest of America to see the outcome of the show and to see who Al ended up with. As she lay down to sleep in the luxurious bed that night, she couldn't stop the tears that fell and were absorbed by the pillow.

Chapter Eighteen

Five months later...

Sam, Beth, and Christina were gathered in Beth's apartment, ready for the season premiere of Love in the Outback. Sam chuckled. They hadn't changed the name after all. It seemed like everyone in Albuquerque knew that Sam was on the show. She'd interviewed with the local news stations as well as radio stations. She'd done her best to talk up the show, but not reveal anything either. She figured if she refused to be interviewed that would keep the interest of the media even longer than if she just gave in and did the interviews. Even though the interviewers wanted to know the outcome of the show and if she was a finalist, Sam was prohibited from saying anything by the contract she's signed. Eddie and the other producers made it very clear from the start that if she let any information leak out about the outcome of the job she'd be sued for millions of dollars.

The three friends decided they'd rotate whose place they watched the show at each week. Beth and Christina were beyond excited, Sam was definitely not. She knew that watching the show would bring back memories, mostly bad, but bitter sweet too. She wasn't sure she wanted to watch the "behind the scene" shots of Al's dates. She didn't want to see what went on that she didn't know about. She was interested to see how they edited the show, though. She knew that many people who were on so-called reality shows

187

complained about the editing. She couldn't think of anything that she'd done that would embarrass her or make the editing difficult, though.

Even though several months had passed since she'd seen Al, she missed him. It seemed like every night she lay in bed thinking about him. Where was he? Did he miss her? Did he think about her? She was embarrassed to admit that she thought about him while pleasuring herself as well. She remembered everything about their date and the kiss they shared. That kiss was better than any sex she'd had with anyone else. That was almost embarrassing because she had no idea if Al felt the same way.

The show had a cutesy opening, complete with music and pictures of all the women. Sam's head shot was toward the beginning of the montage, it was only on for a few seconds, but none of the women had theirs up for long. The show started at the hotel with the women frantically searching through their bags, trying to pack what was needed. It continued with the video introductions for Al. The camera kept panning from the bus driver to the women. Sam laughed out loud.

"What?" asked Christina. "The bus driver is Al!!" Sam exclaimed with a laugh. The three women burst out laughing. "Wait, shhhh," scolded Beth as she tried to hear the show.

The show continued on. It showed the women settling into the bunkhouses. Sam thought that overall the show was actually pretty boring. It ended with Wendi's name being pulled out of the cheesy cowboy hat. The cameras milked it for all they were worth and had close up shots of Wendi crying and carrying on and sobbing in her interview in the car.

Hey. Sam thought to herself. I wonder why they didn't talk to me when I was leaving.

The three women laughed at the show and discussed the contestants. Of course, Beth and Christina didn't like any of the women, except for Sam. They laughed at how Sam had to be called "Sammi" and rolled their eyes at how everyone's names ended in the sound of "ie."

Beth commented at the end of the first show, "Sam, where were you? I didn't see much of you at all! Weren't you there?!?" She said it jokingly, but Sam had noticed the same thing. Granted she didn't socialize much with the other women, but there really were only a few shots with her in them.

"I was there," Sam insisted, trying to laugh about it. "I'm sure you'll see my fat butt next week!" They all laughed.

Finally, it got late enough that Christina and Sam had to get back home because they had to work the next day. They made plans for the next week to watch the next installment of the show.

Sam arrived at her house to a noisy greeting from her dogs. Blue, Albert, and Duke were always very excited to see her. Most of the time they just slept, but it was always nice to have an audience to listen to her ramblings. It made her feel less lonely. They were especially glad to see her when she got back from the show. Her mom had watched them for her, but it was obvious they'd missed her.

Sam thought about Al. He looked just as good as she remembered. She wished she'd taped the show so she could watch it again and see Al. He was just so good looking, and now that she knew what a good person he was, he was even better looking in her eyes. She sighed and wished things were different.

The next day at work was pretty crazy. Everyone wanted to talk to her about the show and how they'd seen it. They had a ton of questions about what Sam thought about the other women, and of course they all wanted to know who "won." Sam, of course, couldn't tell them anything, so she politely fended off the questions. She had two calls from local reporters who wanted to interview her and she made appointments for the next day. Around three in the afternoon Sam looked up from her desk to see a giant bouquet of flowers making its way toward her desk. Okay, it was actually the receptionist carrying them, but it almost looked like they were floating on their own.

The receptionist placed them on her desk and said, "Delivery for you."

Sam couldn't imagine who they could be from. She wasn't dating anyone, it wasn't her birthday, and it wasn't any kind of special day. Sam leaned over to smell the beautiful blooms. They were a mix of several different kinds of flowers. There was a lily, a carnation, a rose, some baby's breath and some other flowers that Sam didn't recognize.

The receptionist hadn't left and nosily asked, "Who're they from?" Sam looked for a card. There wasn't one.

She shrugged and said, "I have no idea, I can't find a card."

"Who sends flowers without a card?" the receptionist asked almost rhetorically. "Maybe it fell off, I'll look for it. Maybe it's a secret admirer who saw you on TV last night, or maybe it's Al!" she said animatedly. Sam could tell she really liked that idea.

"I doubt it," Sam told her. "I wasn't on the show enough last night for anyone to notice me, and we're strictly forbidden to have any contact with anyone that was on the show. It was in the contract. So even if I *did* win," she paused and winked at the receptionist, playing it up, "I can't have any contact with him until the show is over." Sam smiled to herself. Let her think about that one a bit!

After work Sam carefully put the flowers on the front seat next to her and strapped them in using the seat belt. It wasn't often that she received flowers and she wanted to savor them in private at home. She had no idea who'd sent them. It wasn't as if she saw many people other than the ones she worked with, and there were only a few men at work anyway, and she certainly knew that none of them would send her flowers. She considered throwing them out, but at the last minute couldn't make herself to do it.

When Sam arrived home she put the flowers on her kitchen table. She then fed her dogs and popped a microwave dinner in to cook. She sat down at her table to eat her solitary dinner. She sighed. She was lonely. She had lots of friends, and her dogs to keep her company, but it wasn't the same as having someone at home to talk to and to share the day with.

Susan Stoker

Chapter Nineteen

The next week arrived quickly. Beth and Christina came over to Sam's house this time to watch *Love in the Outback*. Sam knew this was the week when they'd have the fish competition and meet Al. It was interesting watching the show from an outside different perspective. She was there, she knew what happened, but it was weird to watch the editing and see what the producers pulled out of the show. The women got their popcorn and sodas and sank onto the couches to watch the show. Albert was sleeping on his favorite pillow, Blue was on the couch next to Sam, and Duke was curled up on a pillow in the corner.

The theme song came on and the montage of pictures was on again. The teaser this week had many shots of the women looking bedraggled. Finally, the show was on. They saw some background on Al to start with. First of all his name wasn't Al, it was Alex. Sam thought that Alex fit him so much better than Al did. She supposed it wasn't too far of a stretch to believe that Eddie had made him change him name as well. After all, they'd changed hers. She briefly wondered how many of the other women had their names changed too, but her attention quickly turned back to the show. Sam was surprised to learn that Alex wasn't "just" a rancher that the show led them all to believe. It turned out that he was the CEO of his own business in Austin. He did live on a ranch, part of the time. He owned both a house in Austin as well as the ranch. The guy was loaded.

Beth sighed. "Wow, Sam," she said. "He's gorgeous and rich to boot!" Sam hadn't told her friends the outcome of the show. She wasn't allowed to, and besides, they said they'd rather wait and watch the show like everyone else. They said it heightened the suspense. Sam suddenly felt relieved that she hadn't won the show. There was no way she'd fit into Alex's world. She might have been able to fit in on a ranch, but be the girlfriend of a CEO? No way!

The editing of the competition left much to be desired in Sam's opinion. There were, of course, lots of shots of the women soaked with water. Lots of shots of the women bending over head first in the bucket, trying to get the fish out. There were a few shots of Sam, but mostly of the other women. The friends watched as the twist came, the winners had to meet Alex right then and there or wait until the next day. Sam laughed, remembering how mad they all were, especially Missy. She watched as the "winners" were bussed off and the rest of them stayed. It was interesting that there was no mention of her falling into the water or her being wet. She thought for sure her fall into the water would have been played up just to embarrass her, but it wasn't even mentioned. She watched the conversations Alex had with some of the women. They didn't show all of the conversations, she supposed they just showed the "interesting" ones, and of course hers wasn't included.

The show continued with the other women the next day getting to meet Alex. Sam and her friends laughed at the conversation that Al had with Courtnee. They then watched as the competition with the pigs came up to see who'd be going home. It was pretty

194

funny to watch them all running around trying to capture the pigs. Sam was absolutely dumbfounded when, through the magic of editing, *she* was left without a pig instead of Kimmie. They must've spliced together frames of her standing around empty-handed.

Sam couldn't say anything as the "elimination" took place. She watched as she walked towards a car and was driven away. She knew that the shot was taken out of sequence, but she was still amazed. The teaser scenes for the next week's show came on talking about the days spent on the ranch doing the chores. Beth and Christina hung around for a bit longer, commiserating with Sam about how she had to leave so early in the show and they told her that it wasn't fair. Sam barely heard any of it.

After her friends left, Sam sat on her couch, hugging one of the throw pillows. She now understood what all the other reality stars had been talking about when they complained about editing. They'd edited her out of the show even though she'd been there much longer. She wondered how that was going to work. How were they going to get rid of Kimmie since she wasn't at the ranch? She guessed they just weren't going to deal with the shoveling of the barns much since she did most of the work. It must've taken a long time for them to edit her out of all the subsequent shots. She felt betrayed, but she honestly wasn't that surprised. She knew when the cameras didn't follow her on her one and only individual date with Al that something was up, but she tried to brush it off with a flimsy excuse. She knew she wasn't like the others, but she honestly didn't think they'd just erase her from the show.

Finally, after an hour or so of feeling sorry for herself, Sam decided that what happened had happened. And since she couldn't change anything about it, there was no use getting worked up and pissed off. She hadn't won, they didn't change the outcome of the show, just the order that people left. She also decided she wasn't going to watch the rest of the show. As much as she loved looking at Alex and remembering how hot he was and how he made her feel, there was no telling how much other stuff they'd manipulated with their editing. Besides, Sam didn't know if she could stand watching Alex make out with the other women. She still wanted to think of him as hers.

The next day at work was one of the longest in Sam's life. Everyone wanted to know all about the show, and they wanted to tell her how sorry they were that she wasn't able to stay longer. She was even teased by some coworkers for not being able to catch a pig. Sam laughed along with them, while inside she cringed. She'd never ever as long as she lived agree to be on any kind of "reality" anything. It wasn't worth it. Later that day the receptionist came into her office to deliver another package. It'd been a week since she'd received the flowers. It was a flat envelope. Sam opened it and was surprised to see a gift certificate to a National pet store chain. There was a note this time, however.

Sam opened it and read, "Hopefully you can put this to good use." That was it. Sam turned it over to look on the back. There was no name or anything. Sam thought it was very weird. She certainly *could* use the gift certificate. Her basset hounds were constantly going through stuffed toys. They liked to "kill" them by taking out the squeaker. It was an odd gift to send to someone anonymously, but appreciated nonetheless.

The week continued and Sam constantly had to deal with the aftereffects of being on a national reality show. She participated in interviews for the local newspaper and even participated in an interview on one of the morning news shows. She couldn't say much about the show. She wasn't allowed to say anything about who might win, and since Eddie and the other producers edited her out of the part of the show that she actually did participate in, she couldn't say anything about that either. Sam told Beth and Christina that she wasn't going to watch any more of the episodes. She explained to them that since she'd been kicked out so early it didn't matter to her who won, and she didn't care to see the rest of the show. They tried to convince her to watch "just for fun," but Sam refused. If she was honest with herself, it was just too painful.

Her feelings were really hurt by the whole experience. First, she was made to feel as if she was somehow less of a person than the other contestants. Second, no one cared about her at all on the show. Not when she was hurt, not when she's saved Kina's life, and definitely not when they edited her out of the show almost altogether. Then she thought about Al...no, Alex. She stupidly thought they'd connected on their date. They had explosive chemistry even before that, but everything he did for her and to her on their date just cemented her feelings. She didn't think he had anything to do with getting her kicked off, but now that it was so much later, and her feelings were so raw, she wasn't sure of anything anymore. She wouldn't put herself through watching him interact with the other women on the show and having it proven to her that she was just another contestant to him and he was going and saying the same things to everyone.

The next few weeks went by and Sam received regular updates from her friends about what was happening on the show. She heard all about the ranch episode. Beth laughed herself silly at some of the girls trying to do their chores. They were both appalled at Kathi's fake drowning. It seemed like Eddie and the other producers knew all along she faked her accident and decided it made good television. Sam felt sick when Christina had told her how the camera zoomed in on Kathi winking to Courtnee and played it in slow motion over and over again. It sickened her and made her want to hunt Eddie down and beat the crap out of him because she knew that Alex must be watching the show and seeing he'd been made a fool out of on national television. She wouldn't wish that betrayal on anyone. What she went through seemed like nothing compared to this.

Occasionally she would see blurbs from the morning news shows about the show and she caught a few interviews with some of the contestants. They didn't start interviewing the women until there were about eight left.

I guess those of us who left in the beginning of the show just weren't worth it. Sam thought to herself.

Throughout the weeks the show was on Sam continued to get little gifts. After each show she received something. She'd received gift certificates to restaurants, another bouquet of flowers, the deluxe edition of the movie *Speed*, a pass to the local zoo…it was mostly all unusual stuff. There was never a name on who'd sent any of it. One week Sam actually called the flower place that delivered the flowers but the customer paid cash and didn't leave his name, so that was a dead end on trying to figure out who was sending the gifts.

Sam wished she knew who it was so she could thank him or her. They really made her feel good, especially after hearing the rundown of the show each week. It seemed like the show was a huge hit and everyone was talking about it.

But another part of her was completely freaked out. Not knowing who was sending the gifts was a little freaky. She thought that maybe Beth or Christina were sending the gifts, but when she asked them they both denied it. Sam knew them well enough to know they weren't lying. So who knew her well enough to send such personalized gifts? She hoped the next reality show she'd be on wouldn't be one where women talked about their stalker.

* * *

Soon enough weeks went by that the season finale was to be aired. It was down to two women for Alex to choose from. Beth and Christina begged her to come and watch the last show with them. Finally, Sam agreed, just to get them off her back. She might as well. Nine months had gone by since she'd left the show. It wasn't as if Alex was knocking down her door, and he couldn't even if he wanted to because of the contracts they'd all signed. Sam knew the final two

199

women were Amy and Kathi. She couldn't believe that Kathi was still there. She hoped for Alex's sake that he took the advice she'd whispered to him that last day she was there.

The show started with the montage of pictures like usual. It then recapped the last week's episode where Missy left the show. The women were now staying by themselves in their own camp sites. The producers had separated them, of course, for dramatic effect. The women had one last individual date with Alex before he'd make the final decision. Kathi and Alex were flown to a nearby town where they had a romantic dinner, complete with candlelight. After dinner they took a carriage ride around the town. They then went back to a hotel where they were given the option of staying in one room together. Of course Kathi was all for that. She and Alex spent some time snuggling and kissing on the couch in front of the television in the room and then the last shot was of the two of them walking into the bedroom hand in hand.

Sam felt sick. She knew she shouldn't have watched the show. She just knew something awful like this was going to happen. Of course, the editors left enough doubt as to what was going on in the room for the audience to make their own conclusions. And the truth was, no one had any idea of what happened. God, it hurt. She wanted to tear Kathi's hair out at the same time she wanted to crawl into bed, put the covers over her head and not come out for weeks.

The final date with Amy was much the same. She and Al went out to eat, then spent some "quality" time together and were then given the option of staying the night together. After some heavy kissing on the couch, the two of them went into the bedroom together.

Beth and Christina were loving every minute of the show. They debated whether or not Alex had slept with either of the women and they were trying to decide which he should pick at the final ceremony. They knew he'd felt really sorry for Kathi after her "near drowning" and it looked like he felt responsible for her. On the other hand, Amy was a strong woman and, in Beth's and Christina's eyes, she was the prettier of the two. The added twist to the show was that the audience knew Kathi lied about the water incident, but Alex didn't. It made for a suspenseful ending.

Sam got up to refill their soda glasses as Alex was debating on which woman he should choose. He was lying on his back on a sofa in a hotel room, talking out loud to himself. He talked about how he thought Amy was beautiful and since she was from El Paso they lived closer to each other. She was an outdoorsy kind of girl and they got along really well. Kathi, on the other hand, was very fragile in Al's eyes and he loved feeling like he could take care of her. She was from Knoxville, which wasn't that far away really, and besides, since he was a pilot it wouldn't make that much difference.

As much as Sam didn't want to admit it, she was as sucked into what was happening on the show as Beth and Christina were. The show changed venues to a beautiful set with the Australian sun setting in the background. Alex was wearing a tuxedo and looked so good. Goose bumps rose all over Sam's arms as she watched the show. He was so good looking and she regretted not being able to be his.

Finally, Robert came onto the set and began to talk

to Alex. He asked Alex if he'd made his decision.

Al responded, "Yes, Robert, I believe I have, I think I knew what my decision was from the first week."

Sam thought that was really odd and a huge blow to her ego. If he knew he wanted either Amy or Kathy from the first week what was he doing with her? Was what he'd told her that last day they were together a lie? She tuned back into the show.

"It was a tough decision, all the women were wonderful and I feel lucky that I've been able to get to know them throughout the past weeks. Tonight I'll make the only decision I can. I was once told I had to trust in my decision, and so tonight I will."

Sam wrinkled her brow…did that mean that he was going to trust *her*? She'd told him to trust her that last day. She was so confused. He had to pick Amy, he just *had* to.

Kathi and Amy were brought out to where Robert and Al stood. They both were beautiful. They had their hair done in dramatic upsweeps and their dresses were worthy of any runway in Hollywood. They were very striking standing next to each other. They were both tall and very slender. Finally, Alex made his speech.

He talked about how this was the hardest decision he ever had to make. Sam laughed, all contestants on reality shows said that in situations like this. Alex continued to talk about how he thought he'd made the best decision he could. He looked at the women.

"Please know that whichever one of you I don't choose, it wasn't because you aren't a good person. You're both beautiful and I know you'll have no problem finding someone back home. The woman I choose is…" he paused dramatically. "Kathi."

Sam nearly choked on the soda she was drinking.

"No way!" Beth exclaimed. "Why did he pick that bitch!?!?"

It was a great ending to the show. Sam had to admit, even though she was crushed. Kathi rushed forward and grabbed Alex around the neck. She squealed with delight. She had tears coming down her face, but Sam noticed that somehow she managed to still look beautiful. The camera panned back to Amy, she looked forlorn standing by herself. As part of the show, Alex walked her to the car.

The cameras showed Amy looking up at Alex and asking, "why?" as if her world had just ended. Alex gave Amy a big hug. It looked like he was whispering in Amy's ear, but the microphones couldn't pick up his words since they were just too low. Sam couldn't help but remember the way he'd done that to her too and how his mouth felt on her ear that day on their picnic. Her stomach lurched a bit.

Finally, he let Amy go, kissed her on the cheek and helped her into the car. It looked like he took a big breath and made his way back to Kathi and Robert. Kathi rushed into his arms again, while Robert made a speech about true love and how Alex had made his choice. As the picture faded out, Alex and Kathi were dancing to a romantic ballad. Kathi was looking up into Alex's face and running her hand through the hair at the back of his neck.

"Ugh," Christina grunted. "That was disgusting. Why did he pick *her*? She wasn't nearly as nice as Amy was. What a disappointment. I thought your Alex had better taste," she finished.

"First of all," Sam started, "he isn't *my* Alex. Secondly, he didn't see all the footage that we did here at home. He had no idea what she was really like, she was completely different around him. And I guess he's just the kind of man who doesn't like a strong independent woman. He'd rather have someone to take care of, I guess," she finished glumly. That was what was really bothering her. She just couldn't believe Al would rather have someone like Kathi than Amy. She'd tried to tell him, maybe he thought she was jealous or something. She should have told him about Kathi's fake accident when she was there. If Sam couldn't have him, she didn't want Kathi to manipulate him and make him miserable either.

Beth shrugged. "No matter what the reason, it'll be a great interview on the morning news show in the morning. Now that he's seen the show and the footage about her, I wonder if that will change anything."

"Probably not," Christina said. "He seems like a forgiving kind of guy. I bet it won't matter to him. I always wonder if they've had any contact since the filming ended. I mean, isn't it in the contract that you can't have contact with the winner in case it leaks out, Sam?" she asked.

Sam nodded. "Yup, I had to sign a contract specifically saying that if I was the last woman I wouldn't contact him by phone, letter or in person until the final show aired." Secretly, she wondered if the feelings on any reality show winner's part could stand nine months apart or if they snuck around and talked anyway. She thought she'd heard about other couples from other reality shows that had met in secret before the show finished airing.

Chapter Twenty

The next morning Sam was running late. She'd forgotten to turn on her alarm the night before because she'd cried herself to sleep. She wasn't able to get the picture of Kathi and Alex dancing cheek to cheek out of her head. Besides that, Beth and Christina hadn't left until late and she'd already been exhausted, physically and emotionally. So she was late getting up and had to take the quickest shower of her life in order to have time to feed and walk her dogs before she had to leave for work. Because she had no time, she wasn't able to watch the morning news channel that was going to have Alex and Kathi on.

Sam rushed into work only a few minutes late. Because she didn't want to irritate her boss she went right to work rather than talking to her co-workers first. As she was in the middle of answering an email to a client, she received a notification on her computer that she'd just received an email. She opened it up and didn't recognize the address it came from. The email said only:

Did you enjoy the gifts?

Sam looked around quickly...could it really be from the person who'd been sending her all the gifts? She was a bit leery, but responded immediately.

Who are you? She typed, not answering the original question and hit send.

You really don't know? Came the response.

Sam looked closely at the email address...Xander546@yahoo.com...it could be anyone.

I wouldn't have asked if I knew. Sam quickly typed and hit send again. It was actually sort of fun to have an anonymous pen-pal.

You didn't answer my question, did you enjoy the gifts? The sender asked again.

Of course I did, who wouldn't? Sam typed back, not sure what else to say to this stranger.

The next email popped up immediately. *Did you watch the news this morning?*

What a strange thing to ask. Sam thought. *Nope, didn't have time, I was running late, what did I miss?* Sam asked, wondering for a moment if there'd been some terrorist attack she'd missed or something else just as big.

It took a while for a response to come back, but when it did Sam read, "Watch the news, then we'll talk."

"What the Hell?" Sam said a little too loud. How could she watch the news when she didn't record it on her DVR? Sam figured that Xander546@yahoo.com was male, but she supposed it could be anyone. She decided that maybe she'd go to a National News web site and see if anything struck her as odd. She was about to type it in when her phone rang. *Oh well, maybe later.* Sam thought as she got back to work.

It turned out there was a crisis at work that day. Sam didn't get to leave her desk to talk with her coworkers at all. Her boss asked her to take care of a nasty situation with a client and Sam spent her entire day talking to HR, the client and then to her boss as well. They had to come to some sort of compromise so the attorneys wouldn't get involved. As she was leaving work, her cell phone rang. It was Beth.

"Where are you?" Beth said as soon as Sam answered.

"I'm leaving work, where are you?" Sam asked.

"I'm at your place, hurry up and get here…did you see the news this morning?" Beth asked.

"Why is everyone asking me that today?" Sam responded grumpily. "No, I was running late, why? What was on it?"

"I taped it for Christina because she called this morning and said she couldn't watch it. She's coming over to meet us at your house. Hurry up and get here, I think your neighbors are getting ready to call the cops on me!" Beth told her.

Sam laughed. She did have some pretty nosy neighbors. "I'll be there in ten minutes," she told Beth, starting her engine.

When Sam got home Christina had already arrived and both she and Beth were impatiently waiting.

"I heard all about it at work," Christina said, "I can't wait to see it for myself."

Sam was now really curious. First the email, now her best friends.

"What the hell is the big deal?" Sam asked as they entered the house.

"I can't believe you have no idea!" Christina told her. "It's the interview with Alex and Kathi! I heard it was great!"

Now Sam was confused. Was that what the email sender was talking about?

"What else was on the news this morning?" Sam asked, thinking that maybe there was something else going on in the Nation that she should know about and that pertained to the morning's emails.

"Who cares!" Beth practically shouted. "You *have* to see this!"

After letting the dogs outside, Sam sat down on the couch while Beth fiddled with the tape. Finally, she got it going. The three friends sat back to watch. The news anchors, David and Jenny, were doing their bit about the upcoming segment. They discussed Alex and Kathi and how they would be coming right up. When Beth taped the show, she obviously edited out the commercials, because the next scene was Alex walking onto the set with Kathi. She was grinning from ear to ear. She still looked beautiful. She had on a short black dress and her hair was down around her shoulders. She was hanging onto Alex's arm like she'd fall over if she didn't have him to hold her upright. Sam thought she was even skinnier than when she was on the show! And Alex, holy crap, he looked great. He wasn't wearing jeans like he did for the show. He was wearing a business suit. It looked different, but still wonderful.

The couple walked in and sat down on the couch in front of the news anchorwoman Jenny.

"Welcome, Alex and Kathi," she said enthusiastically. "It's great to see you. How are you both doing? Is it true that you haven't seen each other since the show ended?"

Kathi immediately answered, "It's true. But it's as if no time has gone by for us." She looked up at Alex and continued. "I'm just so thrilled to be able to be with him in public now." She gushed.

"Jenny," Alex interrupted Kathi, "I agreed to come here today because my contract says that I had to." With that gasps were heard from the studio audience, even Jenny, a seasoned reporter looked like she didn't know what to say. Alex's tone of voice left no doubt he wasn't a happy man. When Kathi was about to interrupt, Alex continued.

"I've watched the show along with the rest of America and have seen things I didn't know were going on while the show was being taped. Because I feel as if I was deceived, I don't think like I need to continue on with this farce of a relationship. I could never be with someone who wasn't honest with me. I hope that everyone can understand and hopefully they support me in my decision. I'm sure that Kathi…" and with that he turned to look at the woman sitting next to him, who was staring at him in shock, "will find a man out there who'll be perfect for her in every way. I honestly don't believe I'm that man."

Jenny asked him quickly, sensing he was about to stand up and leave, "Is there someone else?"

Alex looked at her, then looked at the camera. "I hope so, if she'll have me."

With that Alex stood up, kissed Jenny on the cheek, and walked off the set. Jenny then, apparently still in shock, wrapped up the segment without giving Kathi a chance to defend herself or protest and the program cut to a commercial.

"Holy Cow!" Christina said. "That was better than a soap opera! I'm so glad he left her skanky butt! But I'm sure the network executives are having a cow!"

"I don't know," Beth responded slowly. "This is great publicity. They probably didn't expect that their final woman and Alex would stay together anyway, and they'll get more leverage out of this than if they'd stayed together."

Sam couldn't say anything, she was in shock. Alex had sounded so calm and confident in his little speech. He didn't sound heartbroken at all. She couldn't understand it. Wasn't he embarrassed? He chose Kathi over Amy, wasn't he upset about it at all? She thought about it for a bit while Beth and Christina continued to speculate about Alex and Kathi. Suddenly, a small smile came over her face.

"What?" Beth demanded. "You have the weirdest look on your face."

"He played them," Sam said. "Just as they played him. It was brilliant. No wonder he owns his own company!"

The three women just laughed. Finally, Beth and Christina left. Sam asked Beth if she could keep the tape. She watched it three more times. The look on Kathi's face was priceless. Alex didn't look brokenhearted, he looked triumphant. She was a bit crestfallen about the fact that he already had another girlfriend, but at least he didn't end up with Kathi. She didn't think she'd be able to stomach that. The last thing Sam thought before she went to sleep was if she'd hear from her mysterious email pen-pal the next day. Was that interview what she was supposed to watch?

Chapter Twenty-One

Sam arrived at work early the next day. She eagerly opened her email. As she'd hoped, she had an email from Xander546@yahoo.com.

It was an invitation to talk over an instant messaging program. Sam already had the program on her computer since the company used it to talk to each other. She quickly added Xander's email. As soon as it was added she heard a "ping." She'd received a message from Xander.

Did you watch it? was all it said.

Sam responded, Yes. What part are you referring to?

The Love in the Outback Section.

I saw it.

What did you think? Xander replied.

I thought it was a smart thing to do, Sam responded, not knowing who she was really talking to. It could be a reporter looking for more information, or it could be a producer trying to get her to break her contract somehow.

Why? Xander asked.

Look... Sam typed I don't know who you are or what you want. How did you get my email anyway? Why are you sending me things? This is getting a little creepy. She was getting a little freaked out by the whole thing. She wasn't sure what Xander wanted and how he'd gotten her information.

I'm sorry. Xander typed I mean you no harm, I was just curious as to what you thought about the

211

situation. Would you feel more comfortable if we met in person?

Sam paused. She was interested, but she was also a bit scared. She must have paused too long.

I don't mean to scare you. Xander typed. We can meet wherever and whenever you want. It can be at a fast food restaurant for all I care, but I'd like to meet with you. I think it'll clear up a lot of confusion on your part. I know it's not fair of me, but I ask you to trust me.

Sam thought she must be crazy because she typed back. *Okay, this weekend? I'm not sure where…*

Xander quickly typed back. Great! You won't regret it, I promise. How about the tram?

The tram? Sam asked.

Yeah, why don't we say Friday night, at the top of the tram off of Tramway Blvd, 8pm. Then once you hear what I have to say we can either have dinner or you can leave.

Sam had always loved the tram. She didn't like the trip to the top in the tram car much, but it was so beautiful at the top of Sandia Peak. Looking over the city it almost made up for the scary ride up there. *Okay, how will I know who you are?* she asked.

You'll know, Xander responded. Until then.

With that Xander logged off of the messaging program. Sam immediately called Beth to tell her what she'd done. Now that she'd agreed to meet whoever this Xander was, she was scared to death. Beth, however, was thrilled. She was sure it had to be a man, someone who'd seen her on the show and was in love with her and finally got up the guts to ask her out. Sam wasn't sure. The entire situation was odd, and she wasn't sure she wanted to get into a relationship with anyone. It was hard enough getting over Alex, and they didn't even really have a relationship in the first place!

Later that day Sam received another package. This one was from one of the local department stores. When she opened it, it was a pair of princess cut solitaire diamond earrings. They weren't that big, maybe half a carat, but Sam was still shocked. Like usual there was a note, but it didn't say who it was from.

Please wear these this weekend. It would please me to no end.

Sam had never received anything so beautiful in all her life. She wasn't sure she should accept them, but she didn't know who to return them to. She'd always wanted a pair of diamond earrings, but figured it was too big of an expense to splurge on for herself. Figuring she'd be meeting a man that weekend rather than a female was now almost a certainty.

Friday night came pretty fast. Sam had planned with Christina to call her about eight-thirty on her cell. It was a typical ploy that they came up with when going on a blind date. Christina would pretend to be a neighbor and say that one of her dogs had gotten out and that she had her at her house and would Sam please come and get her. That would give Sam a chance to leave if she wanted to.

Sam looked around the parking lot at the tram station. She didn't recognize any of the other cars. She didn't like coming alone, but there were plenty of other people around. She bought her ticket, then hung out in the small gift shop until her tram arrived. She got on

213

with the other passengers. As the car started its slow ascent, Sam wondered for the hundredth time what she was doing. She had worn the earrings. They were beautiful and she couldn't imagine not wearing them. In fact, she'd been wearing them all week. They'd most likely become her new "everyday" pair. Sam had taken great pains to dress up tonight. She wanted to look nice, but not *too* nice considering she wasn't sure about Xander's motives. She wore a black pair of pants and a lime green turtleneck sweater.

After about twenty minutes the tram finally docked at the top of Sandia Peak. Sam let the other passengers push their way out of the car while she tried to look around to see if she recognized anyone. She slowly made her way out of the car and toward the small building. She didn't see anyone who looked like they were looking for her so she entered the building. Most of the other passengers obviously had reservations at the restaurant and were making their way toward it. Sam stepped in and looked around. There were two children with their mother and some other people waiting for the return trip down to the tram station. Sam walked further into the building. Around the corner, she saw a man standing by the windows on the north side, looking out. Sam looked around. She didn't see anyone else around. When she turned back toward the man he'd turned so he was facing her.

Sam couldn't believe her eyes. It was Alex! What was he doing here? All she could do was stare at him in confusion as he walked toward her.

Alex approached Sammi. She looked beautiful. He couldn't believe it'd been so long since he'd seen and talked to her. It was almost as if it was the same as the day they parted. Alex thought the confused look on her face was cute. He reached out to take her hands.

"Sit with me?" he asked with some trepidation.

Sam could only nod. Alex led her over to one of the benches alongside the windows. Sam sat down and Alex took the seat next to her.

"What are you doing here?" Sam asked with her brow furrowed.

"Sammi," Alex started "I—"

Sam interrupted him. "Actually, my name is Sam," she told him, blushing lightly.

Alex smiled. "I'd wondered about that. I knew your email said that was your name, but I thought that maybe you went by Sammi. I should've known. My name isn't Al either. It's Alexander David Sanders the third."

Sam finally smiled. "I heard that when the show aired. That fits you much better than Al. Do you go by Alexander? I feel like I don't know you at all."

Alex smiled. "You know me, Sam. We weren't together very long, but I think we got to know each other pretty well. I go by Alex."

"Alex, okay," Sam told him. Suddenly, a thought struck her. "Xander in your email...short for Alexander, huh?" She smiled at him.

"I wondered when you'd figure that one out," he told her.

"I don't understand, Alex." Sam's voice trailed off.

"I know, and I'm sorry. I wanted to explain to you," Alex said. "And I did promise you'd hear from me again, remember?"

215

Sam nodded, but didn't say anything. Her head was reeling. She couldn't believe Alex was here, apparently for her. It blew her mind.

"You know about the contract I was under because you were under the same rules. I wasn't allowed to contact anyone from the show until after it was over. It said I couldn't write, call or see anyone, it didn't say anything about sending things." Alex smiled. "I'm sorry about the show, Sam. It wasn't fair what they did in the editing to you. I called and cussed out Eddie after that second show. I don't think he really cared since the show was doing so well, though. Frankly, I was surprised they were able to do it so well. But I'll tell you one thing, I'm not sorry for—" He paused.

"What's that?" Sam asked him, leaning toward him and putting her hand on his arm. She sighed. It felt so good being able to touch him again.

"I'm not sorry that our date wasn't shown on National TV. That kiss we shared would've melted televisions around the country." He smiled at her.

Sam looked at him sadly. "I felt the same way, Alex, but after seeing you on the finale…" Her voice trailed off. How could she explain to him what it did to her to see him being intimate with Amy and especially Kathi?

Alex looked her straight in the eye. "Sam, if I could, I'd take it back. I was getting a lot of pressure from Eddie to step it up a notch. What you saw was for the cameras. After we went through that bedroom door we went our separate ways. I swear to you what you saw was all we did." He waited anxiously for her response.

Sam looked at Alex. He looked very earnest. "I

believe you, Alex. I know how they edited me out of the show, and I'm sure it was easy to make the audience think you did something you didn't. But honestly? I don't know why you're here and what you want from me."

Alex stood up and took her hand. "Please, I'd like the opportunity to talk to you more. Will you have dinner with me?"

He looked so sincere, Sam stood up and squeezed his hand. "Of course, Alex, I'd love that."

They walked hand in hand down to the restaurant at the top of the mountain. Alex had already made reservations in the hopes that Sam would agree to stay there with him. As they were waiting to be taken to their table, Sam's cell phone rang. Knowing exactly who it was, Sam blushed as she answered it.

"Hello? Oh, hi. Uh huh. Yup, no problem. Okay, see you later." She hung up and looked at Alex, who was smiling from ear to ear.

"Problem?" he asked, laughing. Sam had an idea he knew exactly what had just happened.

"Uh, no, everything's fine," she said, trying to act nonchalantly.

Alex threw his head back and laughed some more. "I'm glad you want to stay, and I don't blame you for coming up with a contingency plan."

Sam blushed some more. Luckily, right then the hostess came back and led them to their table. It was located right by the windows that overlooked the city. Alex held Sam's chair for her, then unexpectedly sat down next to her rather than across from her.

"Is this okay?" he asked.

"It's great," Sam told him earnestly.

The waitress came by and they ordered drinks. Alex turned toward Sam and took her hand in his again. "I don't know where to start," he said honestly.

"I know," Sam began, "it seems as if we just met yesterday, but we know each other better than a usual blind date couple would. I know things were pretty intense in Australia."

"They were," Alex agreed, "but there are things you don't know about our time over there that I feel like I have to tell you."

Sam started to look and feel nervous.

"Nothing bad, I promise, but I told myself if you agreed to meet with me I'd be honest with you and I want to do that. I honestly feel like there's something between us. If I'm wrong, please tell me now before I get too far involved in this."

Now Alex looked nervous. His thumb was smoothing over the back of Sam's hand absently, sending shivers down her spine, only making her want him more.

"I feel the same, Alex," Sam told him quietly. "There are things that happened in Australia that I'd like to share with you too."

"I get to go first." Alex insisted with a smile.

The waitress came back and they ordered their meals. Sam knew the restaurant was expensive, but Alex didn't seem to care about the price. After some more small talk their meals arrived. They took their time eating. Sam seemed to enjoy the meal more than she ever had before eating at the top of the mountain. Perhaps it was the little brushes of her arm against Alex's, or maybe it was the small talk they engaged in. Whatever it was, it made the meal almost magical.

Finally, after they both finished their meals, Alex said, "I don't really know where to start, but I did want to tell you that I had nothing to do with you going home or the editing of the show."

"I know, Alex." Sam reassured him for a second time. "I never thought you did. I figured you were as much in the dark as the rest of us were."

"The fact is, though," Alex continued nervously, "I was consulted and asked on many occasions who I wanted to leave. I chose the first five or six women who went home. Including the very first one, it wasn't a random thing."

"How is that possible?" Sam asked. "We hadn't even met you yet!"

"I'm assuming you watched the show, right?"

"Some of it. I really only watched the first couple shows and the last one," Sam admitted reluctantly.

Alex would have teased her, but he was too intent on telling her everything about the show. "Remember, I was the bus driver, I made the decision based on first impressions."

"That's right, you saw all of our video introductions live and in person." Sam blushed, remembering her video. "Man, I was a dork!"

"On the contrary, I thought you were very refreshing. After listening to the other women talk about where they liked to shop and go out at night your story about the bus was precious." Alex reassured her. "Eddie asked me who I wanted to go home, I told him and they rigged the outcome. On the day you went home, Eddie told me you were going to go. I begged him to let you stay. He tricked me. He promised me that Cindee would be going home that night, but he didn't say for certain that you *wouldn't* be."

"It's okay, Alex." Sam soothed him. "I knew that given the choice, any of the other women would choose me to leave. I just didn't fit in with them. And I know I didn't fit in on the show."

Alex leaned over and kissed her gently, cupping the side of her face with his palm and keeping her face close to his. "The other reason I knew who I wanted to go home was because I was allowed to see all the tapes from the camp and from the competitions and stuff when I went home at night." Alex explained.

Sam stared at him. What was he saying? That he'd seen everything they'd done at the camp? "What do you mean?" Sam asked confused.

"Just what I said, Sam, I saw you fall in the river and not complain one bit. I saw the scrapes on your side from that fall. I saw you save Kina's life with that snake. I saw the conversations that everyone had back at the camp, I saw everything…"

Sam could only stare at him. "W-w-what do you mean?" She stuttered, feeling stupid.

Alex pulled her close again and rested his forehead against hers. "I mean just what I said. I think I fell in love with you after that first night. You were freezing, but you never complained, never brought attention to yourself, never told anyone you were hurt. Beauty in a woman I can take or leave, but true courage, pure unselfishness gets me every time. When you saved Kina's life and didn't bring it to the attention of anyone else, not a lot of women would have done that. And let's not even start to talk about the barn incident. Why didn't you tell my aunt and I what really happened?" he asked her firmly, leaning back and mock glaring at her.

"Your aunt?" Was all Sam could manage. She was dumbfounded with all that Alex was telling her. She couldn't wrap her mind around it all.

Alex chuckled. "Yeah, Nancy is my aunt. We watched all the tapes together and she helped me decide who was leaving. You impressed the hell out of her, you know. We didn't know what really happened in the barn, but we could make an educated guess. But without you telling us for sure, we couldn't say or do anything."

"I did it for selfish reasons, Alex," she told him honestly. "If I'd said anything they would've made my life a living hell. I was able to do it, it wasn't a big deal. I felt pretty darn proud of myself."

"Ah, honey," Alex murmured, bringing her palm up to his mouth and kissing it tenderly before continuing. "That's not selfish, it's self-preservation. I just wish you didn't have to get hurt in the process."

"So you saw all the tapes every day?" Sam asked, trying to take his mind off of the barn.

"Not all of them. Eddie got pretty sneaky and started leaving out the most interesting ones..."

"How did you know they were leaving some out?" Sam asked.

"Kina would bring them to me. I think you made quite an impression on her," he told her. "She'd bring me the ones that Eddie was leaving out on purpose."

Sam stared at him. "I had no idea. I was afraid she didn't like me since I almost got her killed with that snake. Then when they weren't filming me much anymore I figured that was why."

"No, Sam," Alex continued, "You were her

favorite from day one. I think she was as mad as I was when you left."

Sam could only stare at him, overwhelmed.

"I saw the tapes from that day at the lake as well. I had no idea Kathi was faking it until Kina brought me the tape. I saw the wink that night, Sam. I knew Kathi was lying. I knew she didn't almost drown. I about lost it. I wanted to quit the show, but I was under a contractual obligation. Besides, Eddie wouldn't let me kick her off. I tried. God, how I tried. He said it made for good television…and ultimately he was right."

"But, but, I don't understand why you chose her at the end then," Sam said with confusion. "If you knew the whole time, didn't it matter to you?"

"Of course it mattered. It was hard for me to even be civil to her. You said you didn't watch much of the show, but did you see any of it after the lake competition?"

"Honestly? No. After the second episode when they twisted everything around I had no desire to watch. My girlfriends made me watch the last episode with them. I didn't see anything in between."

"I don't know whether to be pleased or irritated," Alex told her with a grin. "While Eddie told me that I had to keep Kathi around I did my best to not have her win individual dates, and I certainly didn't help her that much while she was 'recovering'," Alex told her. "As to why I chose her at the end? I heard what you told me while we were on our date, and I honestly liked Amy. But if I'd picked Amy I'd have no reason after the show ended to dump her. I didn't want to hurt her. By choosing Kathi I had a perfect excuse to dump her on National Television and use the information the show provided as my reasoning."

"I don't understand, Alex," Sam said, "If you'd chosen Amy you could've made that work. She was pretty nice, and I know you got along, and she's from Texas, you could've made it work!"

"Sam," Alex said quietly and intensely, "I didn't *want* it to work. I knew the day you left that *you* were the one I wanted to make it work with. Do you remember what I said the other day on that morning news show?"

Sam could only shake her head in confusion. Had he really just said he wanted to be with *her*?

"I was asked if there was someone else, and I said I thought there was. That someone else is *you* Sam. I want to make us work. I know we'll have some obstacles in front of us, but I haven't stopped thinking about you since you left the show. I go to sleep wondering what you're doing. I dream about meeting your dogs. I can see us mucking out my barn together." He smiled. Then said, "Please say something…" he trailed off.

"I'm not really sure *what* to say," Sam told him honestly. "I like you too. I guess that's part of the reason why I didn't watch any more of the episodes after they edited me out. I know how I felt that day on our date, but I figured there was no way I'd fit into your world anyway." Sam saw the irritated glint in Alex's eyes and quickly continued. "Don't get mad, Alex. I know as CEO of your company you have to project a certain image, just as I know I'm not that image."

"Don't sell yourself short, Sam," he told her. "I'm a person just like you and just like everyone who works for my company. Are you telling me you think they'd rather have me be with a person like Kathi who would lie her way through life?"

"No, that's not what I'm saying," Sam said with exasperation. "I meant that you should have someone by your side that is beautiful and thin and—"

Alex cut her off and grasped her arms, looking into her eyes. "*You* are beautiful. Why won't you believe me? I've never liked bony women. There's nothing to hold on to." He winked at her. "You're beautiful, Sam. You're beautiful in part because of who you are. You make me happy to be around you. I love your long legs, your eyes sparkle with life…there isn't anything about you I don't think is beautiful. I'd rather have you by my side than any of those women on that show. I thank my lucky stars every day you were in Australia, I'm not sure we ever would've met otherwise. Please tell me there's a chance for us. I want to date you, Sam. I want to get to know you here in our own little corner of the world. I want to take you out to eat, to the zoo, I want to hang out with you and your dogs and watch movies on the weekends. I want to hear about your day when you get home and be able to tell you about mine. I want to spend all day in bed with you, exploring your body and making you come apart under me. Do you think we can try that?"

Blushing because she'd thought about having Alex in her bed as well, she managed to say, "But we live so far apart," Sam hesitantly told him.

"Did you forget I'm a pilot?" Alex grinned at her. "You think I'm going to let a few miles stand between us?" He got serious and stared into her eyes. "I'm not saying it'll be easy, Sam. All I'm saying is that I want a chance. I want the chance to make you happy. If down the line we decide together we should make our home here in Albuquerque, we will. If we decide Austin is where we should live, we will."

At Sam's surprised look, he continued. "I'm in this for the long haul, Sam. I want us to end up together, married, together for the rest of our lives. This isn't a short-term fling for me. I want us to go into this expecting that we'll make it permanent. I'm not promising anything, things might not work out, but I want you to know that I'm serious here. I've had nine months to think about this, about us, and even though we weren't physically together very long, I've watched those tapes from the show over and over and I've missed you terribly…please let me know what you're thinking behind those beautiful eyes."

Sam looked at Alex. He looked so earnest, so worried. She lifted her hand and smoothed it over his brow. "I want those things too, Alex. I never expected to find someone like you. I'd like to try."

Alex leaned in and caught Sam's lips with his own. He couldn't be gentle. He slanted his head to the side and ravaged her mouth. God, she tasted so good and all he could think of was laying her down and spending all night exploring her body. They spent the next few minutes lost in each other's kiss and only came up for air when they heard the waitress clearing her throat next to the table.

"Did you need anything else?" she asked with a grin.

"No, I have everything I need right here," Alex replied, never taking his eyes off of Sam. "I'm the luckiest man alive."

Susan Stoker

"No," Sam replied. "*We* are the luckiest people alive."

Epilogue

Sam and Alex were lying on the couch, watching a movie. Sam was lying with her head in Alex's lap and his hands were idly brushing through her hair. The last year was like a dream. After Alex had come to Albuquerque to get her the media frenzy was unbelievable. The newspapers and entertainment shows had gone crazy over the story of the reality show hunk who ended up with one of the rejected contestants.

They'd dated for a few months, but Sam quickly realized there wasn't anything keeping her in Albuquerque, except for Beth and Christina. They wouldn't let her stay for them. They wanted her to be happy and they loved Alex. Alex made it a point to include them in something every time he visited. Sometimes they all went out to dinner and other times they just hung out at Sam's house and watched movies. As a result of his efforts to include them in their relationship, they were the first to tell Sam to move to Austin.

They sat down with her and had a long talk. The three talked about Sam's relationship, they talked about what would happen with Sam's career, and they talked about sex. Anytime the three of them got together the talk most often turned to sex.

Sam wasn't one to talk much about what she and Alex did in the bedroom, but she'd admitted to her friends that Alex was incredible. She hadn't been a virgin when they'd gotten together, but he made her feel inexperienced. He was patient and the two of them together were explosive.

The night Sam told Alex that she was thinking about moving to Austin was amazing. Alex showed her his appreciation for hours in her bedroom. It hadn't taken him long to arrange to have her belongings moved into his ranch outside of Austin. Albert, Duke, and Blue were happy to move to a bigger house as well. They quickly acclimated, but then again, they were happy anywhere Sam went.

Blue was currently lying at Sam's feet on the couch, while Duke and Albert were napping on one of the many dog beds strewn about the room.

Alex's cell phone rang and Sam looked up as he leaned over to answer it. She only heard his side of the conversation.

"This is Alex. Hello, Eddie. Good. Really? Congratulations. What? Uh, I'm not sure. It's not about the money, Eddie. Hell, you know we don't need it. All right, I'll talk to her and we'll think about it. Yeah. You too. Bye."

Sam watched as Alex ended the call and put the phone back on the table next to the couch. His hand returned to stroking her hair. Sam waited, knowing he'd tell her what the call was about when he was ready. There was no telling what Eddie wanted now. Sam really couldn't hate the man. After all, he was one of the reasons she was with Alex now, but she also knew how the man operated. He never did anything out of the kindness of his heart.

Finally, Alex took a deep breath.

"That was Eddie."

Sam nodded and sat up, snuggling into Alex's

side.

"He wanted to let me know he's starting a new reality show based in Arizona." Alex shook his head and chuckled. "He wanted us to come to the set one day to meet the contestants and encourage them with our story."

Sam laughed. "He does remember that I was kicked off and he arranged to edit me out of the entire show, right? What kind of encouragement will our showing up offer anyone?"

"Maybe that they too can make it out alive?" Alex said sarcastically.

Sam laughed. "You decide," she told Alex. "I don't care what we do. I've got you, you've got me and he can't do anything to break us up."

"Damn straight," Alex said.

"I do feel sorry for whoever is on that show, though," Sam said. She squealed as Alex suddenly stood up, cradling her against his chest.

"Those poor bastards," he agreed, nuzzling against Sam's neck, breathing in her scent. He carried her up the stairs to their bedroom. "I suppose we should make an appearance to keep Eddie off our backs. You know he won't give up if he wants us there."

Sam barely managed a nod as Alex leaned over and placed her on their bed. She had much better things to think about than some new reality show that Eddie was planning. She had to think about how she'd please her man.

The End

Susan Stoker

About the Author

Susan Stoker has a heart as big as the state of Texas where she lives but this all American girl has also spent the last fourteen years living in Missouri, California, Colorado, and Indiana. She is quite the romantic and even met the love of her life on "Hotmail classified" before online dating and sites like match.com even existed!

Susan has been reading romance novels since middle school and once crossed out the names of the main characters in a book and changed them to her own and to the name of her crush. She's been writing scenes for years, developing her unique writing style.

Susan loves writing but her true passion is adopting dogs from rescue groups and shelters. Susan and her husband have had a total of nine "rescued" dogs since 2000 including a variety of basset hounds and bloodhounds. She has recently branched out and adopted a basset/terrier mix who acts more like a terrier than a basset (i.e. digging, eating a couch and being hyper). If you love romance and want to help her support adopting great dogs, be sure to check out her work listed below.

The first series, Beyond Reality, is a trilogy, with all three books in the series having Happily Ever After endings with no cliffhangers.

Connect with her at
www.facebook.com/authorsstoker
or
www.facebook.com/authorsusanstoker

Happy Reading!

Made in the USA
San Bernardino, CA
20 August 2014